ALDEBAR HOME

TERESA HOWARD

This is a work of fiction. Names, characters, places, and incidents are products of the author's imagination or are used fictitiously and are not to be construed as real. Any resemblance to actual events, locations, organizations, or persons, living or dead, is entirely coincidental.

World Castle Publishing, LLC
Pensacola, Florida
Copyright © Teresa Howard 2022
Paperback ISBN: 9781958336014
eBook ISBN: 9781958336021
First Edition World Castle Publishing, LLC, May 30, 2022
http://www.worldcastlepublishing.com
Licensing Notes
Cover: Olivia Pro Design
Editor: Maxine Bringenberg

TABLE OF CONTENTS

PROLOGUE
—ALDEBAR PRIME—NELLARI HOMELAND
People of Magic and Stones
Third among the Aldebarian peoples
to sign the Peace Accords.

Porthiea's house squatted like a toad at the end of the narrow forest path, almost hidden by trees and brush. Even the night crickets stilled as Galandra passed. Flickering yellow light shone through the windows, welcoming visitors to the healer's home. A carpet of red and brown leaves led to the door, filling the air with the earthy smell of their decay. The wood was quiet except for the rustle of small creatures scurrying in the dark. Modern observers would deem the mud-brick walls and thatched roof centuries out of date. Tell those same people they were in the Nellari homeland, and they would nod in understanding.

The woodland animals grew still, focusing on the house as if something momentous was happening. Inside, the two women, friends of over fifty years, argued in front of a stone fireplace. The flames blazed brighter as their words flew across the room, illuminating the pale blue walls and simple furnishings. The argument went on.

"Dangerous, yes, but there is no other way," Galandra insisted. "I'm not getting any younger."

The crackle of more logs catching fire punctuated the

silence. Her words hung there, waiting for a response.

"Sixty-two is middling age. Nellari are a long-lived people," Porthiea countered. "Besides, there is another way." The woman Galandra called Porthy was even older and had been her personal healer for thirty years. Turning her back on Galandra and rummaging through jars and tins that contained a wealth of herbs and powders hid her tears and anger. Finally, Porthiea held up a jar and shifted it toward the firelight, straining to read the label.

Galandra sighed. There was no way to hurry Porthiea's search or her comments. Connection to the power-grids had been available for years, but she refused to abandon fires and oil lamps.

Finally, Porthiea seemed pleased with the selection and shifted back to the discussion. "A ship will leave for Earth in three dawnings, and there will be a special envoy on board. For stones sake, Galandra, you are a member of the High Council. Send a message. Make inquiries!"

Galandra tossed back heavy dark hair, a single band of silver shining in the firelight. Days of fasting had etched fine lines in her face, and her mirror had screamed her advancing years. There would be time for rest and feasting later. Determination straightened her tiny frame. "I don't trust spaceships, or envoys. I trust magic. The stones have power."

"The stones have power," Porthiea echoed. She put a packet of thoil leaf, its sweet, sharp scent escaping the bag, into Galandra's hands. She enclosed Galandra's thin hands with her own. It was a liberty few dared take with the high priestess of the Nellari people. "What if it breaks the stone?"

Galandra flinched. It was surely an ill omen for Porthiea's words to echo her own fears. "There are reasons you don't understand, Porthy."

Porthiea's hands clung to hers as if she feared letting go would allow Galandra to be swallowed up in a dark sea. "How much of it is revenge? You can't bring him back."

"I can call her home. She belongs here." Galandra turned away. She wanted to cry, but there was no time for tears or memories. She straightened her back, stretching tired muscles, and steeling herself behind the role of high priestess. "If I am not back by breakfast, come to the Chamber of Stones. I will need a healer."

The corners of Porthiea's mouth drooped. She took the hem of the apron tied around her ample waist and wiped her face. She sighed heavily, turned her back to Galandra, and tidied the kitchen.

Galandra wanted to reach out, embrace her old friend and explain, but she couldn't. The moons were already high in the sky, and much depended on this night's work.

The path to the Chamber of Stones led up a rocky slope behind Porthiea's house. It wasn't far, a short walk for a young woman, longer for one past her prime. Galandra stopped once, bracing her hands on her hips to catch her breath. She had made this climb many times, could have made it even without the moonlight. The night air soon chilled her skin and soothed her bruised spirit. She could forgive Porthiea's harsh words. If this worked, she could forgive almost anything. Night creatures stilled their chatter in solemn respect as she passed. She straightened as her destination came into sight.

Once inside the Chamber of Stones, Galandra lit a fire upon the altar and laid out the tools of magic. She was ready, and yet she hesitated. Perhaps Porthiea was right; maybe this couldn't or shouldn't be done. She had never summoned this magic before. No one had taken such a risk. She would sacrifice Allia, a living stone, one of the stones of her ancestors. What if she pushed the magic too far, and it broke beyond the power of the other stones to save it?

The voice of her own sweet stone, Bajir, drew Galandra out of the cloud of dark thoughts. *Allia knows the risk. She volunteered for this honor. She is not afraid. Hurry now, or there won't be time before dawn.*

Galandra bowed, offering each element of the sacrifice to the fire. First, powder like soft white snowflakes drifted over the flames. Next, the thoil leaves filled the air with fragrant smoke as they were added a handful at a time. Drawing a sharp blade from the pocket of her robes, Galandra made a quick cut across her palm. With her hand over the flames, the blood fell into the fire like crimson raindrops. Finally, she added the stone, Allia. Rising from her knees and settling cross-legged before the altar with her head bowed, the high priestess waited. Minutes, then an hour, she waited, her senses filled with the smoke of burning leaves and blood. The power of the stone began building, slowly at first but then faster. As the power increased, it overtook her, and she could feel the heat of the fire on her body. Her heart quickened and sweat began rolling down her back. Her body shook violently. The weeks of planning and sacrifice came to a shuddering climax in two simple words. *"Come Home!"*

CHAPTER ONE
—EARTH—AN UNDISCLOSED LOCATION

"Come Home!"

The words pierced her dream like a javelin hurled across space and time, dragging her from the nightmare. Kelli woke with a start, the taste of smoke searing her throat. The summons echoed in her mind. She gasped for breath and tried to jump up, but the sheets had twisted around her body during the night. Wrapped like a cocoon, she fell and hit the floor. The impact sent a wave of agony through her shoulder. Pain doused the embers of the nightmare.

She lay panting and stared up at the ceiling in her room, willing her mind to clear. This had been the same dream; an often-replayed nightmare. The men, the fire, Poe's jeering voice calling her a monster—those were the same. But the final command was new. A rush of thoughts filled her mind.

Come home? I have no home. It was just a dream, a crazy dream.

Kelli disentangled herself and tossed the cover back on the bed in a messy heap. No doubt the maid would wonder what had happened during the night. The hardwood floor felt cold and smooth through her thin nightgown. *If this is any sign of how my day is going to turn out, maybe I'll spend the day reading in bed.*

She rolled her ankles and flexed her feet before leaning forward and stretching. Pent up energy sent jittery waves though her body. There was no point trying to go back to sleep. Belatedly, the house AI inquired, "Do you require assistance?" Unless there was an emergency, neither Eric nor the servants disturbed her privacy. If only nightmares and memories were as polite.

"Everything is fine," she assured the unit.

Kelli rummaged in her closet and selected a trendy, metallic sweater that left one shoulder bare and tied at the waist. If she had to avoid the public, she could still follow the fashions. After a steaming shower, Kelli dressed and left the sanctuary of her room. At the end of the hall, the lights and sounds of the game room uttered their siren call. *Not today, we have work to do.*

The high-security computer center that she dubbed Eric's Lair was in the subbasement. It was the center of her life, the one she had made for herself. Her stomach rumbled as she entered the elevator. There would be pastries in the lair, and something healthy too. The mirrored walls whirled in a funhouse effect, elongating her thin frame and distorting her face. On the other wall, she was a munchkin with curly hair. Eric thought this funny, but she found it mildly annoying. She didn't want to see her reflection; it was no longer her. She tried to bring an image of the old Kelli to her mind, and failed. She couldn't remember what she had looked like when she first came here.

Kelli left the elevator and palmed in at the panel that granted entrance to the workroom. The door beeped twice before sliding open. The aroma of coffee and fresh pastries wafted out through the widening gap. Her stomach did a happy dance. Eric sat studying a bank of screens, a mug of coffee and a half-eaten plate of food cluttering his workstation. His head never turned from the flowing stream of information. He looked like a normal middle-aged man, with curly red hair shot with gray. His nose was his only feature with a claim to beauty. It softened his heavy brow and widened his small, hazel eyes. Looks are often deceiving. He was brilliant, her surrogate father, and so much more. He was her savior, mentor, and friend. *Has it been five years since he rescued me from Poe's clinic?*

"Morning, Princess, you're up early. Momma Rosa delivered a superb fruit salad with fresh mangos and bananas this morning to go with the pastries." Eric used his pet name for her, because her character in the game Wizard's World was a princess. His eyes never turned from the bank of monitors in front of him, and his long fingers flew across the keyboard.

She walked up behind him and scanned the monitors. She frowned and reached out to tap the third one on the center row. "We can't do that."

"Why not? It's easy work, and they'll pay out the nose."

She sighed. Eric wasn't deterred by legal issues. How could she explain? Eighty percent of their work was legal in most countries, the other twenty percent was "interesting." He liked the interesting. Unfortunately, interesting had several major corporations and a few governments hunting for him. He loved nothing more than taking down dishonest businesses and corrupt governments agencies. To those who benefited from his secret philanthropic endeavors, he was a hero.

"It's not good business, that's why. You give Saunders Pharmaceutical inside information, and they'll put other companies out of the market." She cleared her throat and added with emphasis, "The cost of your heart medication would triple in a year's time."

"Then everyone's medicine will triple in cost," Eric said, frowning as if surprised not to have foreseen how his actions affected others. He turned and caught her in a bear hug. "That's my Princess, always looking out for me. You always see the big picture and the consequences lurking down the road."

She bit back the urge to remind him she was seventeen, almost a woman, not a child.

"Somebody has to think about consequences. All you

think about is money," Kelli said, and with a gentle shove freed herself. As soon as the words came out of her mouth, she knew they were false. Eric had a heart of gold and powerful sense of justice. He was the Robin Hood of the Cyber World, both criminal mastermind and vigilante for the oppressed. She planted a peck on his cheek. His face felt scratchy with morning stubble and his breath held the aroma of coffee and raspberry Danish. Kelli imagined that was how a father should feel and smell when you kissed him in the morning. If he wasn't her actual father, he had done a good job filling in for the last five years.

She fixed a plate of fruit and cheese, poured a mug of coffee, and settled in for the day. It was 5 a.m. and she joined the world's most wanted info-raider on the information super webs. Eric had taught her well.

Her senses hummed, ready to pounce on even the smallest scrap of profitable information as she scanned the monitors in front of her. After an hour Kelli stretched, stood, and paced around the room. Her body was tense, hyped up, waiting. The longer the day dragged on, the more she sensed something important. She wanted to distract her thoughts.

"Got any information from those linker-chips?" she inquired about one of their latest projects. That she had helped design the technology made her doubly curious.

"It's a work in progress, but I expect nice profits," Eric assured her. There was a smug smile on his face that told her profits would indeed be huge.

"How is the L-7 cognizant program doing?' She fiddled with her keyboard, making conversation.

He turned toward her, ignoring his screens for a moment. His face took on a thoughtful expression. "About ready for human trials."

Kelli nodded and quickly returned to her searches, unable to shake the feeling that something important was going to turn up.

It flittered across the screen like a hummingbird, almost too fast to be seen. She stopped her screen and backed up the tape to be sure she had read correctly. She had. The small one-sentence communications blurb read, "Barringer's Institute has been selected for the Aldebar Project."

What the hell does that mean? What does Barringer's Institute have to do with the Unified Nations World League? And what, pray tell, is the Aldebar Project?

Kelli paused the screen and swiveled her chair toward Eric's station. "My old alma mater is on the UNWL net. You know anything about something called the Aldebar Project?"

"Are you wasting time keeping track of public propaganda pages again?" Although he sounded gruff and sarcastic, his eyes betrayed more than a little interest. He flicked his station to auto-scan.

"Can I do a little snooping?"

Eric nodded. "Be careful. Don't lead those government crazies here. The cost of relocating would be astronomical.

"I know how to be careful."

"That you do, Princess. You also have a lot more to lose if they catch us."

Kelli sighed. "I know, Eric—believe me, I know."

He reached to place a hand protectively on her shoulder. "You're worth over ten of any of them, Princess, no matter who or what your father was. Start digging. I'll bring down the entire government before I let those bastards get their hands on you again."

Kelli grabbed his hand and gave it a quick kiss before turning away to hide the tears in her eyes.

By mid-afternoon Kelli had discovered enough to know that the "Aldebar Project" involved members of the Space Agency, the Defense Department, and some high-level diplomats. This was all remarkably interesting, but not profitable. "I can't go much further without cracking a few security programs. What do you think I should do?"

Eric popped a small disk into her terminal drive. "Read this," he said, his tone smug.

While she had been trolling the waters of the low security information networks, he had been deep-sea fishing in more dangerous waters and had reeled in Moby Dick as proof. The memos told an unbelievable story.

June 26th, 2135...on this date members of a delegation from the Planet Aldebar in the Taurus Star System made first contact. On the advisement of the head of the Security Council, this information has been classified.

"Jesus, that was five years ago. How did they keep a secret so long?"

"Keep reading."

April 29th, 2139...Ambassador Hamilton Davidson became the first interplanetary envoy when he visited Rishal, the Capital of the Degg Homeland, on the Planet Aldebar to establish official diplomatic ties.

Davidson's visit was brief and only partially successful. The Aldebarians proposed an educational exchange involving small groups of teachers and students from both worlds. Barringer's Institute had been selected to provide both.

Kelli's world shrank inside her. The walls of the room seemed to spiral inward. *So, it's happened at last. They've established contact with a sentient alien race. Only it wasn't the first contact. My mother made first contact twenty years ago or I wouldn't be here. Dr. Poe proved that, damn him to hell.*

Eric rubbed his hands together, flexing them as he stretched. "I'm going to put a linker on this."

"A linker? Are you sure? We haven't tested one yet."

He smiled. "Oh yes, I have, and you're a bloody genius at design."

Kelli looked at him with surprise and shivered with a rush of pleasure at the compliment. Eric was seldom given to praise, never flattery.

"Now get back to work. We have made no money today; we can't spend possibilities. Find me something I can sell." Eric turned back to his terminals as the streams of data resumed.

They worked in silence for a while, intent on the bank of screens in front of them and the data flowing by. The computers were programmed to filter the information and alert them if something fit their specifications. But Eric had also taught her that there was no substitute for her own eyes and brain.

"Eric...." Kelli hesitated, and then asked, "Do you ever wonder what your life would be like if things had been different?"

"You mean if they hadn't stolen my Wizard's World game, and I hadn't gotten myself kicked out of school and thrown in jail for trying to fight them? I think about it sometimes. I might have been right here anyway. I sure took to the life once I found it, like a bee takes to honey. I'm happy enough." He looked at her with concern. "What about you, Princess?"

Kelli shrugged and tried to answer without hurting him. "I miss it sometimes; the school, friends my age, not looking over my shoulder all the time. Barringer's was a long time ago, another lifetime, and I'm happy living here with you." She took a deep breath before adding almost in a whisper, "I'm glad he's dead."

She turned away from the pity on Eric's face. Would she ever be able to let go of the past? If she found the truth, could she put it behind her and move on? Who—no, what—had her father been? What had happened to him? Had he been killed in a shuttle crash, or did he return to some distant planet, abandoning his wife and half alien child on Earth?

When she looked up, Eric was studying her face. "What you need, Princess, is another excursion. Let's go skiing in the Alps. I'll be a banker from New York, and you can be my daughter. You can dye your hair red and wear green contacts. You love to ski."

Kelli smiled. Eric was always coming up with excursions that they rarely found time for. "Sounds good to me," she said.

***

A few days later, disaster happened on an old game site. A blue flashing notice announced that Kelli Leigh had a message in Wizard's World Online. She froze. How long had her online persona been compromised? Kelli sat in stunned silence at her terminal, not daring to look toward Eric. Thoughts raced through her mind. How had this happened? Who had succeeded?

Eric swiveled in his chair and gave her a concerned look. "You okay? You're quiet."

"Yes, just need to focus a little. I'll be fine." Kelli turned back to her terminal.

"You're still thinking about that UNWL project. Why don't you get out of here for a while? It would do you good to hang out at the mall like a normal girl."

"We have a lot of work contracted." Her response was halfhearted.

"Don't worry about it. Go find some new clothes or whatever. When we finish these contracts, we are going to take a month off and go somewhere new."

Kelli jumped out of her chair and pushed through the doors of the workroom. She tried to tell herself it was no big deal. It was an old game with an old user-ID. It felt like a big deal. One thing she didn't want to do was lead the Unified Nations of the World League to Eric.

Kelli began the security routine for going outside. She selected golden hair, green contacts, and used a sweet-smelling spray that prevented fingerprints and trace skin and hair cells from identifying her. She had always teased Eric about being paranoid. Today she wished she could do more.

I am not a child. I can take care of this without upsetting Eric.
With that admonition, she exited the garage in her sporty air-car.
It was nothing too expensive or flashy, but it was fast and handled
like a dream. Her first thought was to get as far away from their
home base as possible. That would have to be tempered with
the fact that Eric would expect her back later in the afternoon.
An Airbus station was less than two miles. The flight to Chicago
would take forty-five minutes, and there were several return
flights available. She booked a round trip and boarded the airbus
just minutes before departure.

Kelli made her way down the aisle and took an empty seat,
hoping no one would sit down next to her. She leaned back as the
airbus lifted off and headed southwest. This was as far as she had
planned or even thought. Now with time on her hands, she put
together a course of action. Chicago was a large city — not as big as
it had been in its heyday, but still a sprawling metropolis. There
were plenty of public net-cafés where she could log on using her
old username and see how long ago it had been breached and
trace the person or persons responsible. Kelli was sure it had to
be the UNWL. She dreaded confirming that and having to tell
Eric.

Once in Chicago, she followed information from her
directional device and found a small public net-cafe. The
Connection Place brought back memories of hanging out with
friends after class. It catered to those who wanted a combination
of anonymous online access and live interaction with people.

"Do you have secure terminals?" Kelli asked the pimple-
faced attendant at the host stand.

"Of course, but our secure area has a cover charge."

Kelli nodded and followed him past rows of open terminals
to a smaller area where each terminal was in a soundproof booth.
Her eyes glanced up to an ancient looking clock. There were barely
three hours before she had to be back at the airbus terminal. After
ordering a sandwich and mint lemonade, Kelli sat on the padded

bench and adjusted the workstation. Her eagerness to log on had to wait until her lunch was served and the waiter closed the security curtain. *It's time to get this over with.*

Kelli turned on the terminal and entered the web address of Wizard's World. Taking a deep breath, she entered the username and password. It was an old multiuser game, one that had been popular six or seven years ago, and which held painful and special memories for her. She saw the well-remembered castle and heard the rumble of the dragon from his cave. Her character had nothing to fear from the dragon—she had tamed him long ago. She turned to go to the wizard's castle when a voice came from inside, calling her name, her real name.

"Jesus!" Kelly ripped off the reality visor and threw it against the wall. She had been set up.

On the screen, the game continued an automated journey toward the castle. She could hear the voice faintly calling from the visor speakers. Inside the castle, the game altered again, and a face came into focus. It seemed familiar. Kelli reached down and picked up the visor. She had to listen.

"Good morning, Kelli. I am General Edwards, but you remember me as Colonel Edwards. I visited you at Dr. Poe's clinic. I am sorry I could not get you out of that hell, but I was a lieutenant, and my commander was almost as crazy as Poe." There was a moment of silence, and Kelli's hand shook as she willed herself not to throw the visor again.

General Edwards' face grew larger on the screen as he continued. "Since you have not been apprehended by security, I bet that you are being hidden by a known cyber-criminal. Don't disconnect. I have no interest in capturing Mr. Fendler. Enough money has been wasted on that. In fact, we would like to hire Mr. Fendler, and you." General Edwards appeared to take a drink of water and then wiped his mouth with a napkin. Kelli noticed the sheen of moisture on his forehead. He was nervous or lying.

"When I say we, I am not talking about the Unified

Nations World League. We are all employed by or affiliated with the UNWL but cannot represent the organization in this matter. We have embarked on an interplanetary exchange involving students and teachers between Earth and Aldebar. We need a source of information that is secure. The Aldebarian network is very sophisticated, and there isn't anyone else who has a chance in hell of hacking it. I don't need to tell you how lucrative access to the new markets between Earth and Aldebar will become over the next ten years. If you and Mr. Fendler are interested, please contact me. The address scrolling across the bottom is secure."

After five minutes the screen went black, leaving Kelli sitting in stunned silence. The UNWL was offering her a deal. Was this a way to find her father, or was it a trap?

***

For the next few weeks Kelli tried to hide her obsession with the Aldebar Project from Eric. She was convinced it held the answers to her questions about her father. A plan formed in her mind, sketchy at first and then clearer, until it seemed like her inescapable destiny. She would somehow become a part of this project and go to Aldebar in search of the truth about who or what she was.

Kelli expected Eric to be angry, even hurt by her decision, but she had not expected the laughter and scorn when the truth came out.

"How are you going to manage that? Can you walk back into Barringer's and wave some magic wand and 'poof' they agree to put you on a top-secret government project?"

"The only magic I trust is this." She tapped her finger to her head. "And this." She traced the small metal interface of the newly implanted device behind her left ear and then pointed to the computer in front of her. "I have a plan. If you don't see the profit in helping me, I can and will work with the UNWL alone."

"Since when do you trust these UNWL people? A lot of things could go wrong in this plan. You could be captured or killed, and for what?"

For a moment, she saw the fear in his eyes, fear of losing her, of being alone again in his world.

"More money than even you can imagine in the first five years, and that's just the legal stuff." Kelli tried to keep the desperation out of her voice.

The fear in Eric's eyes was replaced by the shrewdness and avarice that were his constant demons. A linker chip attached to the government transmissions with the Aldebar Project sending back data to Eric would be worth millions of dollars in saleable information. Having her fitted with an intel-7 interface and gathering data on Aldebar was almost more profitable than even he could imagine. He whistled. "I'm in."

CHAPTER TWO
—ALDEBAR PRIME—DEGG HOMELAND
People of Honor and Sand
Second to sign the Peace Accords

A faint ping sounded as the recording ended and a message light blinked to life. The tiny sound, barely audible, was enough to upset the delicate balance needed to maintain a meditative trance.

Shual's body twitched slightly and translucent lids lifted to reveal silvery orbs. His pupils, which normally sparkled like black diamonds in their almond-shaped beds, were mere jagged slits in a hazy silver pool. He let a sigh escape and his mouth slit rippled. A pink tongue flicked out to taste the air. For a moment, the Degg communications officer savored the sweetness of inner peace still fresh in his mind.

The blinking light pounded senses heightened by the power of the Nellari meditation stone. *Is there nowhere in the homeland where one is safe from discord and distraction?* Shual condemned his thoughts as selfish and inefficient. He turned to respond to the message.

Corte, a most junior communications officer, answered the return call. "Forgive this intrusion, most honored senior worker. One did not realize you meditated at this hour."

"There is never a time when duty may not happily call. Speak freely, brother worker. This port is secure."

Corte blinked at the directness of this reply, and Shual intoned a lengthy apology for displaying unseemly impatience.

Corte nodded and began. "Most honored senior worker, this one is happy to report the security scan of our network is complete. It uncovered a breach in one program. The program did not malfunction, but the breach is siphoning information. One hesitates to intrude upon your valuable time, and indeed I have chosen the most inopportune moment to do so. However, you left strict orders to be notified of any anomalies."

"You have done well, brother worker. I am on my way to review the findings."

Shual extinguished the sacred flame and put away the incense and meditation stone. The imported candles and incense had cost him two months' salary, the stone much more. The expense had been of little matter to Shual; one who lived simply and had, of course, other sources of income. If his estimations were correct, which was seldom in doubt, he reckoned himself to be one of the wealthiest Degg in the homeland. He was young, but had been elevated to senior programmer for the planetary communications network, and ran a lucrative trade agreement with the Nellari for the rare blue stones found on his family estate. At first, Shual's interest in the stones was as a source of income for his clan, but now he was a convert to their healing power, and quite an expert on the Nellari culture.

When he arrived, Shual found everything laid out in perfect order in his work area. Corte had also fended off two other senior programmers who desired access to the reports. Shual nodded in satisfaction. Corte was a promising young worker Degg; perhaps it might be possible to elevate him to the position of personal assistant to the senior programmer. They were of an age and worked together well. The promotion would depend on the openness of Corte's mind and, of course, the approval of Rom

Nabbar. Luckily Nabbar was a progressive Rom, and enjoyed the favor of the high lord of Deggar.

Shual perused the report. "You were right to bring this to my attention. What is your assessment?"

"I am a most junior officer, Senior Programmer Shual."

"I know your status, brother worker; I value your opinion here."

Corte's pale gray skin flushed dark silver with pleasure. "I have seen nothing like this, Most Senior Programmer. It is a most atypical design. However, it should not be difficult to remove and replace the breached subroutine. The new security program will prevent any further breach of the network."

"Would that not alert those who placed this program on the network?"

Corte nodded. "Yes, Senior Programmer, it would, but protocol calls for removing the program. Senior Programmer Dashi and Senior Programmer Nobis recommend removing any breached program and installing a replacement with higher security parameters."

Shual studied the young programmer for a moment before replying. "Remove the 45299 communications program and oversee the replacement."

"But Most Senior Programmer, the breached program is 45699."

"I am aware of which program was breached, Personal Assistant Corte. Your report was one of the highest quality, and I gave it my full attention."

Corte blinked and his mouth slit rounded to the shape of the full moon. "I will get right on it, Most Senior Programmer."

Shual's heart fluttered as he watched his newly appointed assistant leave. *I am a most dishonorable Degg,* he thought, marveling at how easily deception flowed from even the purest fountain.

He had completed the request for Corte's promotion when his communications port blinked and Rom Nebbar himself appeared on the screen. Shual became conscious of a lack of neatness in his robes, and hoped this was not apparent onscreen.

"Most honorable Rom, this one was about to send you a report."

"You found the breach, brother worker?"

"Yes, most honorable Rom, one of my most promising junior programmers reported the breach hours ago. I have not examined all the data, but tracking the source of the breach may be difficult."

"One fears we know the source of the breach, brother worker. We need your help to prove those fears."

"I am at your service, most honorable Rom."

"My belief, and the belief of our high lord, is that certain Narr lords are attempting to undermine the authority of the Council of Unity. If they succeed, we may find ourselves back in the times of the Great Wars."

If Shual had not been acquainted with Rom Nebbar, he would have questioned these words, or dismissed them altogether. "A most fearful prophecy, noble Rom."

"Yes, and one that must be prevented at all costs. If we prove that Narr lords are responsible for the recent security leaks, the council will be forced to take action against them, and our alliance with the Shamaru and Bengari will be strengthened."

"Forgive me, Noble Rom, but is this not a matter for the council's security forces?"

"They are looking into the problem and reporting to the full council. You will report your findings to me and through me to our high lord."

Shual hid his surprise. One hoped the council's security forces could be trusted. "Noble Rom, this one is a programmer, not a security officer. There are others who are more qualified."

Rom Nebbar nodded, a note of sympathy in his voice when he answered. "No doubt, brother worker, but you were recommended to our lord."

Recommended? His name brought before the high lord? Shual grasped the table for support. "You honor me, noble Rom."

Rom Nebbar shook his head. "You thank the wrong individual, brother worker. I was, of course, surprised one of my chief programmers was known to the high priestess of Nellar. She requested your help in this matter."

Such honor was overwhelming. Shual tried to speak. He tried to move. He fainted.

CHAPTER THREE
—Earth—Barringer's Institute
A Journey Begins

"It's not my fault your brain can't handle direct input," a tiny voice chirped.

Kelli swatted the interface button behind her left ear, and a sudden ringing pounded in her head. She darted a quick glance around the cruise-bus before sub vocalizing. "Program off."

The miniature hologram disappeared. The visa phone on her wrist bleeped. Kelli smiled and answered with forced pleasantness. "Hello, Eric."

"The L-7 interface went down. Is everything okay?"

"I shut it down. Your hologram has a nasty attitude, and it keeps popping up."

"It's supposed to be self-activated. That's part of the new security subroutine." Eric smiled. "The personality was your idea."

"I said to give it a personality, not an attitude." Kelli couldn't help smiling back. "I'll turn it back on later. I'm on public transportation, and I don't want to explain what I'm doing with a cognizant program."

The cruise-bus came to a gliding halt and a flashing marquee announced Barringer's Institute. The pilot glanced in the rearview mirror, but Kelli's body refused to obey her commands to get up. If she waited much longer, he would move on to the next stop.

I've come too far to stop now. Kelli stood and made her way off the bus. The view of the institute brought poignant memories flooding back. Brick buildings, manicured lawns, and bell tower glittered in the morning sunlight like the ghost of some eighteenth-century ivy-league campus come back to haunt the twenty-second century.

A horn blared, warning her to step away from the curb, and a powerful expulsion of air from the departing cruise-bus threatened to lift her off her feet. Kelli steadied herself, looking across the campus. *This is crazy. I've spent years creating a new life for myself, and now I'm jeopardizing it.*

Unbidden, a thought entered her mind. *You're going home.* She blinked at the absurdity of her subconscious mind. Eric was her family, and the Lair her home. Squinting in the sunlight, she forced her legs to start up the path leading to the administration building. Each step brought her closer to her future or her doom. She wished she knew which.

At the top of the small rise, Kelli entered the building and made her way toward the office of Dr. Karl Granger, president of Barringer's Institute for Gifted Students. Margaret Ashford, his secretary, sat at her desk updating vid-files, as Kelli remembered, down to the smart blue business suit and white blouse.

"May I help you with something?"

Relieved that the secretary did not recognize her, Kelli smiled. "Yes, my name is Kelli Royal. I have a 9:30 appointment with Dr. Granger."

"Yes, I remember receiving your resumé," Mrs. Ashford replied and added, "We are not open for enrollment. The semester has already begun."

Kelli glanced toward the closed door to Dr. Granger's office. "I understand. He's expecting Ambassador Evan's niece."

Mrs. Ashford nodded. "I'll let them know you're here." She spoke into the intercom and then turned to Kelli. "You can go in now."

A fragrant smoky haze filled the office, emanating from an ancient pipe tucked between Dr. Granger's lips. He radiated resentment. She knew they had forced him to have this interview, and he was inclined to dismiss her plan out of hand.

"My name is Kelli Royal. Do you remember me? I was a student here about six years ago, but the name was Kelli Leigh then."

Recognition contorted his face, but he remained silent, whether in shock, disbelief, or anger she couldn't tell. Her eyes darted around the room, and she noticed Professor Michael Gentry. His face radiated shock, but not displeasure. It seemed like an eternity before Dr. Granger spoke.

"I was expecting someone else." His stern expression brought a blush to her face.

"I'm sorry about the deception." Kelli glanced toward Michael Gentry for help, and found none. He was staring as if seeing some ghostly apparition. Taking a deep breath and feigning a casual tone, she unloaded the first volley. "Congratulations on the Aldebar Project, gentlemen. You deserve the recognition."

That bombshell, softly spoken, exploded inside the room. Dr. Granger slumped into a chair. Michael Gentry seemed to recover first. Then with remarkable calm he walked across the room and took Kelli in his arms and squeezed. It was so different from the painful goodbye hug haunting her memory. "Is it you? We thought they had taken you into custody years ago."

"No, I'm still on the lam," Kelli laughed. His genuine affection was more than she had expected or dared to hope.

"I need a moment," said Dr. Granger.

Michael Gentry continued, "The UNWL has classified the Aldebar Project, so this is a bit of a shock, and we have heard nothing from you for several years."

She stood there, allowing him to study her with something akin to disbelief in his eyes. She raised an eyebrow, and he blushed and indicated the ivory divan opposite Dr. Granger's desk.

"Where did you hear about the Aldebar Project?"

Kelli paused before answering, considering the edge in his voice. "I've been tracking the communications between the Unified Nations World League and Aldebar for five months. I'm an excellent spy, for a fugitive space alien."

Michael winced and his face and neck reddened. Kelli wanted to assure him that none of it had been his fault. The government required him to report the anomalies in her genetic tests, and at great personal risk he had helped her escape.

Dr. Granger found his voice and denounced her claims. "Young lady, you can't be monitoring a top secret UNWL project. They possess elaborate surveillance systems and an army of security police."

Years of living with Eric had inured her to such tirades. She looked the formidable Dr. Granger in the eye. "The people I work for are part of the UNWL. They hired me to monitor the project. I'm here to help. Not everyone in the government wants this project to succeed."

Dr. Granger turned to Michael. "I told you I thought someone was following me in New York last week. Get security over here to do a sweep for surveillance chips. They could be anywhere."

Kelli pulled a small device from her pocket and walked over to Dr. Granger. She read the screen. "The chips are in your com-panel, your air cruisers, and in your tie pin. I can take care of these, but it may take a minute to locate the frequency. I'm wearing a scrambler, so what we've said so far has been secure."

Michael nodded and ran a hand through his thick sandy hair, over his moustache, and down the square jaw line. "Where did you get a government surveillance scrambler?"

Not answering, Kellie looked down. She was sure he

didn't want to know. He was much safer not knowing.

He said, "You want to go to Aldebar? Are you on a bloody wild goose chase? Do you think you are going to find your father on Aldebar?"

"How do you know he isn't?" Kelli replied. She was breathing hard and fast, the passion sounding in her voice. "Aldebar is a long shot, but it's my chance to find out who or what my father was, and what happened to him."

Hands clenched and jaw tight, Michael spoke in a calm tone. "This forbids your participation, even if Dr. Granger and I both approve. Everyone must pass a level three security clearance. You are seventeen. You're wanted by the government. The UNWL would be on us in an instant. They would end the project and the school."

"Ambassador Evan's niece has her identity and paperwork in order. I think you'll find that he is eager for her to be a part of this project. I wouldn't be here if I thought I was jeopardizing anything," Kelli replied. She could feel tears filling her eyes, but didn't blink them away. "If you'll listen, I know you can help."

Michael reached out and touched her arm. He studied her face. "That's excellent plastic surgery. No one would recognize you."

"Eric hires the best doctors. Please let me help you."

"You can help by telling Dr. Granger how you got your information about the Aldebar Project."

"Let me use your com-station for a minute and I'll show you." Without waiting for an answer, she walked over to the station and in seconds accessed her own computer and its massive data banks. "Read this, and you'll see for yourself that the UNWL has been withholding information."

Dr. Granger pulled his chair close to the terminal and read the reports, screen by screen. "I was afraid of this. If I find anything that jeopardizes the lives of our students and professors, I'll blow the whistle on the whole damn project myself."

Dr. Granger admitted to being seventy, but his health was robust and his mind keen. After an hour, he cleared his throat and looked at Michael Gentry. "I don't like this at all. Both the UNWL and the Aldebarian's refuse to allow alien ships to enter their space. They've been exchanging envoys off planet, and now they've agreed to exchange teams on Space Station Alpha Three, without even consulting us. The Aldebarians are handling all travel in hyperspace. I can't believe they've kept this from me. These are children, not diplomats or soldiers. What are they thinking?"

Kelli reached out and put a hand on his shoulder. "The Aldebarians don't trust the UNWL, that's why they moved the exchange to Alpha Three. Their ships aren't dependent on a jump port to get to hyperspace and back. You can imagine how much our government would love to get its hands on that technology. The Aldebarians aren't about to let us steal one of their ships."

Michael Gentry, quiet for so long, said, "You linked with their computers? That's not possible without knowing their language."

"Did you have any idea who you were handing me over to? Eric is a well-known cybercriminal. After you rescued me, I went underground with him to hide from the UNWL. We're what you would call info-raiders, your great-grandfathers called us hackers," Kelli explained, though she wasn't ashamed of her work. "We're decades ahead of UNWL technology. I helped to design a linker chip capable of accessing the UNWL's network. Sticking one on a message to Aldebar was a long shot, but it paid off." The two men were staring at her in total amazement. She continued. "Aldebar has seven races of sentient beings. To accommodate the differences, the Aldebarian computer network has worked with systems that are diverse in style and complexity. The Aldebarians changed it to receive the UNWL communications. To be honest, it decoded my chip and established the link itself. Now every time the UNWL sends or receives a message from Aldebar, I get information."

Dr. Granger rubbed his hands together. "Do you think it's safe to continue with the project?"

Kelli breathed a sigh of relief.

The viewer-phone buzzed, and everyone jumped. Margaret Ashford appeared, asking if they were ever going to break for lunch. It was two o'clock. She took their lunch orders and in less than thirty minutes they were enjoying soy-beef sandwiches and potato skins.

Dr. Granger wiped his mouth, eager to resume. "If I go along with your plan, how would you get past the UNWL's security checks?"

Kelli's heart raced with excitement. She swallowed the last of her sandwich and delivered her final bombshell. "My friend on the inside assures me it would be difficult for the current government to explain a half alien girl to the voting public during these delicate negotiations. I think they know more about my father than anyone will admit. Either way, it was easy to buy cooperation. American Ambassador Evans signed my new identity and references. I think you'll find him most eager for his niece, Kelli Royal, to be a part of the Aldebar Project."

"This is not a joyride, or your personal vendetta, Kelli. We're responsible for the lives of students. Their safety must always come before any personal concerns. Are you willing to make such a commitment?"

"Yes, of course." Kelli's excitement was contagious. Dr Granger and Michael were both smiling. She was in.

The sun was setting as she headed for her hotel room uptown. That night she sat on the balcony looking at the stars. Aldebar, the eye of Taurus the bull, wasn't visible in the northern hemisphere in summer. She couldn't see it, but she felt it calling her home.

CHAPTER FOUR
—ALDEBAR PRIME—SHAMARU HOMELAND
People of Air and Mountain
First to sign the Peace Accord.

Galandra stood shivering at the entrance to Lord Travalla's keep. Someone had carved the massive castle into the face of a mountain high in the Shamaru homeland. The beautiful stonework had taken years to complete, and stood as a testament to those her people called Sky Men. She shivered and knocked. Frigid air cut through her thin robes and the marble tiles numbed her feet. *How in the name of the stones does Nellandra stand to live in such a chilly place?*

"Come in. Come in." A tall Shamaru woman, dressed in heavy woolen robes and thick leather boots, stepped aside and eyed her with concern. "You must be here to see Lady Nellandra. If I had known you were coming, I would have met you at the transport station."

"It's a surprise visit." Galandra headed for the enormous fireplace, her body craving warmth. She studied the enhanced flames with disgust. They were fine for heat, but useless for magic. "Tell your lady that her sister requests an audience."

The color drained from the servant's face. She bowed and turned to leave. Galandra's voice, stronger now that she was warmer, stopped her. "It isn't necessary for anyone else to know that I am here. Do you understand, Risja?"

"I understand."

Galandra smiled at the woman's retreating figure. Lord Travalla would be furious that she had used a spell on one of his servants, but she wasn't concerned about that. He wasn't a stupid man. What she had traveled far to tell him was too important to risk.

She turned at the sound of hurrying footsteps. Nellandra was tying the sash of a thick dressing robe about her as she entered the kitchen. Concern shone on her face. She took in Galandra's thin robe and bare feet and shook her head. "Risja, fetch one of my other robes and a pair of slippers. I'll put on the tea."

"There's no life in the fire," Galandra complained. "How can you sleep in such an inhospitable place?"

"I may be old, but I still keep my lady warm at night," an amused voice came from the hall, and then Lord Travalla entered the kitchen still wearing his robe, his wings as yet uncombed. Threads of gray highlighted his dark hair. Age lines etched deep into the still handsome face, gave it character, but his lean muscular body rivaled men thirty years his junior. Galandra envied her sister such a mate.

"Well, little sister, what brings you to us unannounced? We would have met you."

"Bravel," Galandra answered, still enjoying the view of Lord Travalla's half bare chest.

"Bravel?"

"I think she means she flew up on a bravel." Nellandra leaned closer and took a dramatic sniff toward her sister. "Oh yes, I smell bravel."

"In this cold?" Lord Travalla sounded incredulous.

"You won't catch me in one of those metal coffins you call transport shuttles," Galandra answered.

"The shuttles are warmer and safer than riding bareback

in these mountains at night." Lord Travalla shook his head.

Risja came in carrying one of Nellandra's robes and a pair of warm slippers. "They'll be over big, Your Majesty, you being such a tiny woman." She bowed and presented them to Galandra.

Nellandra laughed. "My sister is not a queen, Risja."

"No, Lady Travalla, but I didn't know how else to address a high priestess."

"Lady Galandra will do, or if you must be formal, The DaWakanda Galandra." Galandra took the robe and slipped it across her shoulders. She shook her head at the slippers. "Nellari don't wear shoes."

Lord Travalla chuckled. "Your sister was the same when she first came to us. It's a wonder her feet didn't freeze and fall off that first winter."

Everyone laughed. Galandra sipped tea and remembered the other time she had come here. *Why must I always be the bearer of bad news?*

"You've come a long way, sister. Is the news that important?" Nellandra rummaged in her cupboard and came out with some strong-tasting goat cheese, Galandra's favorite. The flavor would go well with the dark bread Risja had baked.

"Is someone plotting to kill Lord Travalla and ruin the Council of Unity important?"

"Maybe we should talk about this in my office while my wife prepares breakfast." Lord Travalla's voice had lost its humor.

The pair of scorching looks he received reminded him these two quite different women were sisters, and Nellari at that. Abandoning his plan, he poured himself some tea, made a face at the bitter taste, and pushed his cup aside. "Tell us then about this plot on my life."

"It's nothing new. The Narr Lords have sought your death for a long time," Galandra said between sips of hot tea.

"I've heard rumors to that effect," Lord Travalla

acknowledged.

"I've heard no such rumors." Nellandra shot her husband a look that said an inquisition awaited him later.

"Have you designated an heir?" Galandra changed the subject and studied Travalla's face.

"Nothing official, but Adoni Ravon has known for a while I hold him in high regard."

"We both hold him in high regard," Nellandra added.

"His mother was once our Holba's dearest friend. If he had lived, Ravon might have been our grandson."

An image of her beloved nephew, Holba, teased Galandra's mind. Most of what they said was true, and the fact both young people had found other loves no longer mattered. Before he died, they had broken their betrothal so she could marry Lord Ravon's heir. "And your nephew, Lord Rischar, how does he stand in your favor?"

Lord Travalla's smile soured. "A fawning, weak-minded fool, like his father. I wouldn't trust him to tend my goats."

"Good, then I won't be causing a family rift if I tell you he's been plotting with the Narr Lord Gorron to sabotage the project." Galandra smiled. Her brother-in-law was a shrewd judge of character.

"Can you prove his involvement? I would love to bring him before the council on charges."

"Nothing he can't deny." Galandra chewed her lower lip. "And that would let Lord Gorron know we are wise to his plotting."

Lord Travalla studied her face a moment, then laughed. "Out with your plan then, witch. I'm game for a little Nellari mischief. If what you say is true, it serves Rischar well to get caught in your web."

"Name Lord Ravon as your heir and put him in charge of the negotiations. Your nephew can't contest such a declaration."

The smile morphed into a scowl as Lord Travalla gave his

head a savage shake. "He's young. I'll not paint a target on Ravon to protect my skin. If there is danger, we will stop the exchange."

"No, you must not delay the exchange," Galandra replied. "That's what they want. The students from Earth must arrive on schedule." She did not dare say more before she knew for sure.

"What can I do then? I'm head of the council, but I can't accuse other members of treason. We've no proof the Narr are plotting against the council."

"You have honorable friends. So honorable, in fact, that anything they bring before the council will be unchallenged."

Lord Travalla's breath went out in a slow whistle, and he turned to his wife. "Please tell me your dear sister hasn't charmed a Degg into giving false testimony."

Both women laughed and continued to sip their tea without responding.

CHAPTER FIVE
—Earth—Barringer's Institute

A month later, Kelli was filling a cup with rich Belgian cocoa as she studied for her first test in the design theory class. She was once again a student at Barringer's Institute.

"Professor Stevens won't cut any slack on your grade," Michael Gentry warned, a twinkle in his eyes. "As long as you don't point out his mistakes too often," he added. The comment was made as a joke and a reminder that her professors weren't up to Eric's level of design.

Kelli stopped to read a message from Niles Webster inviting her to meet some students later for pizza. The professors often awarded him top of his class in science and math. Niles understood the alternative theory, even if the department head didn't. His application for the Aldebar Project was one of the first, and she hoped they would accept him. Team leaders would send out those notices in three weeks, and they had extended the application period. She sent a quick reply. *Sounds fun. I'll see you there.*

The phone interrupted her study again. *I'm popular tonight,* she thought. When she adjusted the screen to see the caller, she saw it was Dr. Granger. She could see his mottled cheeks on the screen, and his voiced pitched an octave higher as he said, "I need you."

"I'll be right over," Kelli replied. The screen went blank. She jumped, glancing down to make sure the phone was working.

Slipping her feet into a pair of sandals and reaching for a hairbrush, she hurried out of her campus apartment. Halfway down the hall, she remembered she had told Niles she would meet the others for pizza. She sent him a quick apology.

Michael Gentry was in front of the administration building waiting for her to catch up. He nodded, and they climbed the steps to the front entrance. He asked, "What's going on? I had a strange call from Dr. Granger telling me to hurry."

"I don't know. But he sounds upset," Kelli answered. She stretched to keep up with his longer strides. Neither voiced their inner fears. If something were wrong with the Aldebar Project, they would find out soon enough. She was almost out of breath when she stopped to enter the security codes for after-hours access.

Dr. Granger's secretary had long since gone home to her family, a pair of Siamese cats. Her desk was a model of organization, everything arranged and ready for tomorrow. A fleeting image of her own cluttered room entered Kelli's mind, but she pushed it aside. She pressed the com-panel to alert Dr. Granger. The green "enter" light flashed on the door.

"Good, you're both here." Dr. Granger waved them in. Doughnuts and coffee were waiting on the table. He had strewn files across his desk and a calendar lay open beside them. They showed a late night of work ahead. He smiled and blurted in a shaky voice, "Our friends at the UNWL fouled things up this time. I'm afraid the Aldebar Project could be over."

"Tell us what's going on." Kelli reached out to Dr. Granger and took his hand. She wanted to calm him, despite her own apprehension.

"They've moved the departure date up six months. As of today, we must select and prepare students for the team by

November. If we can't make the new schedule, all funding for the project will stop and the program scrapped."

"Then we'll make the new schedule. There has to be a way." Michael's calm, authoritative voice was reassuring, but his eyes had darkened to a midnight blue. He poured a cup of coffee and took a deep swallow. He looked up with a blissful smile. "I know things are serious when you bring out the excellent coffee." He turned to Kelli and added, "It's made from beans grown by a South American friend of Dr. Granger's."

"How many applications have we received so far?" Dr. Granger asked.

"Margaret counted fifteen applications yesterday. Another twenty-five are still out," Kelli replied as she filled her own cup with coffee and refilled Dr. Granger's. "We can call the students and have them return the forms as soon as possible."

Dr. Granger nodded in satisfaction. "Get them back by Friday, and background checks on everyone." He paused before making the next request. "I don't approve of spying, but someone is trying to sabotage the Aldebar Project, and I want to know who and why. Ambassador Evans, our sponsor, does not know who pressured the finance committee into this. Can you use your connections to find out anything?"

"Sure, I can handle that," Kelli answered, more than a little surprised, and impressed that the crusty old bird was familiar with what an info-raider did for a living. "What about my classes?"

"I'll give you an excuse for missing classes the next three days. You can use the terminal here. Michael and I will interview an applicant in Australia." Dr. Granger sounded feisty and confident again. He grinned at their puzzled faces. "We need to find another professor for the Aldebar Project."

"I thought we were going with Professor Berryhill?" A bite of doughnut muffled Michael's voice. He washed the pastry down with coffee.

"That's the other bad news. Professor Berryhill is getting married. He withdrew his application this morning. The idea of three years on another planet doesn't fit into his marital plans," Dr. Granger said, and took a swallow of coffee before continuing. "I'll need you to fly to Sydney with me tomorrow."

"Who's in Australia?" Michael and Kelli asked.

"Duncan Meddars teaches at a small-gifted school in the area. He's not happy at the school, so he might be interested in a position on the Aldebar Project. I was thinking of hiring him to fill in for Berryhill."

"Doesn't Meddars promote radical ideas about the psychic abilities of gifted students?" Michael asked, "We don't want such radical thinking here."

Dr. Granger bristled. "Don't be closed-minded, Michael. Meddars is young, but he is a brilliant professor. I've followed his research, and he is no crackpot."

"I don't think we need that kind of research at Barringer's Institute," Michael snapped back. He paused, then added, "I don't know enough about his qualifications to comment, sorry."

Dr. Granger replied, "Quite right, you've no reason to. I was going to discuss the change with you this week, but when the UNWL moved up the departure, there wasn't time."

Kelli interrupted the awkward exchange. "Let's stay together on this. We don't know who wants this project to fail, or why. Four months is precious little time to make this happen."

"I despise doing this in a rushed, haphazard manner. It goes against my nature," Dr. Granger said, and glanced at Michael. "I hope you'll come to Sydney with me to interview Meddars. We can fly back late Wednesday. If all goes well, we can review the applications next week and notify the top candidates. Maybe Kelli will know who we're up against by then."

"I'll do my best," Kelli said. She dreaded digging through Mrs. Ashford's office. "Where does Margaret keep the applications?"

"They're on vid-file in the black box on the bookshelf. She plans on working on them next week," Dr. Granger answered.

Michael and Dr. Granger worked until 1 a.m. before calling it a night. They confirmed their flight to Sidney the next morning, and would return in three days. Michael touched her shoulder as he left. "Better get some rest. We'll see you on Thursday."

"I'll finish here in a few minutes," Kelli said, and focused on the screen. She rubbed her tired eyes and looked at the screen again. *By the end of the week, exhaustion will make thinking difficult.*

Kelli attached a scrambler to the visa-phone. She wanted the help of an expert. The phone line buzzed and buzzed.

Waking Eric Fendler up in the middle of the night took a lot of nerve.

"Hmm?" a sleepy male voice answered. The viewer remained scrambled.

"Who loves you, baby?" Kelli enjoyed teasing Eric. She couldn't suppress the giggle in her voice.

"Princess? Damn girl, it's 3 a.m. Are you okay? Is something wrong? I warned you about going back."

"I'm okay, but need your help."

A crashing sound punctuated by a curse answered her. After a moment of noisy shuffling, the com-screen cleared, and Eric's face appeared. "Help? You said everything's fine."

"I can't fix all the technical difficulties from here." Kelli tried to sound casual.

Eric laughed and smoothed his unruly hair. "You're a poor liar, Princess."

"Ouch. That hurts," Kelli said, and tried to sound offended. "I need a favor, and I get insults."

"Always at your command, Princess, as long as there's a little profit in it."

"Thanks, Eric, I can always count on you," Kelli replied, avoiding the mention of profit. She began feeding him her requests, a bite at a time, the little things first. "We need background files on the families of several students at Barringer's Institute. We can't access their files from here without being traced."

"Those will be ready later in the morning." Eric waited a few moments for Kelli to answer. "And?" His bushy eyebrows raised in inquiry.

"Well.... I need a copy of the genetics program used at Stanford University. I'm sure that Dr. Greenberg designed it. He's good." She watched for a reaction.

Eric's face flushed and his voice raised an octave. "You want what? That won't be cheap. What else do you need? You want the president's diary log or something?"

"Hilarious." Kelli never liked to deal with Eric when he was being sarcastic, but there was no time to wait for him to be in better spirits. Drawing a deep, calming breath, she broached him with the final, most crucial request. "I need to know who pressured the UNWL finance committee to move up the departure date for the Aldebar Project." She adjusted her camera, making her face loom close and intent in his com-screen. "Find out who wants the project scrapped."

"They have moved it up? They're freaking morons. If they cancel the project, I'll lose millions." Eric became all business, his pecuniary interests foremost in his mind. "I'll find out who's behind this and teach them a thing or two."

"Calm down, Eric. Find out who is behind this, but don't blow our cover."

"As if I would, Princess. You did the right thing calling me. I'll send the background profiles later today. The genetics program will take a couple of weeks. Dr. Greenberg designed his own security, and it's exceptional. This UNWL deal is very dicey. You're the expert on their system, can't you do it yourself?" Eric typed notes into his memo log as he talked.

"That would be too risky. Someone could trace back to me," Kelli answered. She yawned. "I need to go now. You can reach me at this terminal until Wednesday. Take care of yourself,

Eric, and try to get some sleep." She blew him a quick goodnight kiss before terminating the call.

Kelli glanced around Dr. Granger's office. It was late, and she was too tired to go back to her room. The divan offered a good place to curl up and catch a few hours of sleep before the background profiles arrived. When she woke, Ms. Ashford had arrived and covered her with a coat before starting a fresh pot of coffee in the antique percolator. An incoming transmission startled her, and she hurried to answer it.

CHAPTER SIX
—ALDEBAR PRIME—NARR HOMELAND
People of Dark and Power.
Sixth of the Peoples to sign the Peace Accord

Ubal bowed his massive head and tried to control his trembling limbs. The sight of the great Narr, Lord Gorron, frightened him. The fear made it almost impossible to walk. Lord Gorron didn't like loose ends, and was famous for sending underlings on suicide missions. For this reason, Ubal strived to prove himself loyal and indispensable to Gorron. Now Gorron seemed ready to put Ubal to the test.

Lord Gorron turned his head to breathe in the acrid smoke of incense burning on the table near him. His chamber was enormous, dimmed by smoke and furnished with dark wood. The walls were crowded with macabre paintings of torture and brutality. They had designed the room to put visitors at a disadvantage.

He waved a withered arm toward a chair. "Sit, Ubal, it's your counsel I seek today, not your worthless life."

Lord Gorron's laugh was not a pleasant sound. He was aware of his reputation, and more than a little proud of the effect it had on underlings.

Ubal straightened and shuffled over to the nearest chair,

adjusting his neck on the head support. "How might my lowly counsel be of service?"

"Shamaru High Lord Travalla refused again to relinquish his position on the Council of Unity." Gorron's voice dripped with venom.

Ubal responded to Gorron's familiar lament. "Yes, but not even Lord Travalla lives forever."

"As long as he lives and has power, he will protect the hybrids," Gorron snarled.

"As will his chosen successor," Ubal reasoned.

"Lord Rischar is weak, and he cares more for his comfort than the welfare of the hybrids, or his own people," Gorron said, contempt for Rischar's weakness clear. He intended to exploit it to wrest control of the Council of Unity from the Shamaru alliance.

"What of Lord Ravon? Is he no longer Travalla's favorite?"

"We must discredit Ravon and make it impossible for him to succeed to the Council of Unity." Gorron pounded his frail fist on the table beside his chair. "I can manipulate Lord Rischar. That will assure us control of the council and do away with the hybrids. Rischar must succeed Travalla."

"Perhaps Lord Ravon could meet with an accident," Ubal suggested. "There are those who could arrange it, for a price."

"Dead, Lord Ravon would become a martyr. I want him dishonored. Lord Travalla will have to step down from the council in shame." Gorron growled as if years of bitterness and hatred had sharpened his desire to destroy Lord Travalla into an insatiable hunger. "You will take care of Ravon for me."

"Yes, my Lord Gorron." Ubal brought his hands together in acquiescence. He knew well that Gorron had trapped him. There was no way to decline Gorron's request and live.

Satisfied, Gorron added, "I will reward you." He tossed a small purse on the floor before Ubal.

"To serve you is my life," Ubal smiled, rising from his chair. At least Lord Gorron always paid for his dirty work.

"No, to fail me means your life," Gorron corrected, laughing at his own wit.

Ubal did not laugh. The words sent a chill down his crooked spine. Gorron saw his fear and laughed even more.

Stumbling from Gorron's presence, Ubal counted himself cursed. If he failed, he would die. If he succeeded, Lord Travalla's friends on the Council of Unity would no doubt seek vengeance. Gorron would kill him to cover his tracks.

You must prepare yourself against Lord Gorron's plans, an ancient voice whispered in Ubal's mind. It was one of the many voices of acquisition he had inherited. Lord Gorron had inherited more.

Another voice hissed in Ubal's mind. *Lord Gorron does not listen. He feels he is above the voices of knowledge.*

A plan formed. If Ubal dared to defy Gorron, it offered a chance for success.

CHAPTER SEVEN
—EARTH—BARRINGER'S INSTITUTE

Four months later, icy rain swept across the campus at Barringer's Institute. Students dashed from building to building trying to protect their electronic notebooks from the rain. The gusts were so strong that conventional rain shields failed to keep out the cold and wet. Shivering, Kelli rubbed her arms as she watched them from her office window. It was early March, and time had passed. Soon, a new era in education would launch from Cape Canaveral.

With Eric's expert help, they had selected nine students and three alternates for the exchange program. He had also produced the name of the problem on the U.N.N. finance committee, Ambassador Telnovka. Dr. Granger was ecstatic.

Kelli's face furrowed into a frown. The cloud on her otherwise sunny horizon came in the person of Assistant Professor Duncan Meddars. Kelli was at a loss to explain his cold behavior towards her. Duncan and Michael Gentry were working well together despite the rocky start. Duncan was outgoing and popular with the other students, but more reserved with her. Kelli fumed. *He initiates no conversation with me, and seems to avoid me like the plague._*

For weeks Kelli had been attempting to break through

his reticence. However, the harder she tried to get to know him, the more Duncan seemed to pull away. Michael said she was overreacting, imagining the difference in the way Duncan treated her. Margaret Ashford advised her to confront Duncan Meddars and air out their differences. Kelli wasn't sure what to do. She felt ignored. She felt slighted, and it infuriated her. Three months was a long time to spend in the close quarters of a spaceship with someone who gave every sign of disliking or not trusting you. Still, confronting the charismatic Duncan Meddars was a frightening prospect. He had an eerie way of looking inside her, reading every thought with suspicion and disapproval.

Kelli decided it was best to brave the proverbial lion in his den. She had done a background check on him, and would love to find out about his theories about psychic abilities. However, that was not the most interesting fact she had uncovered. He was young, twenty-one to be exact. Was that why he was being so standoffish? She grabbed her mauve rain shield and headed resolutely for Duncan's apartment. She stopped twice, almost turning back. The rain was cold and fierce, and she did not know what to say. Still debating, she stood on his doorstep. Running her tongue across her lips, Kelli took a deep breath and pushed the doorbell.

"One moment, please." Duncan Meddars' rich baritone voice flowed from the door speaker. It sounded happy and relaxed. The door slid open, and surprise registered on his face, then anger. He hadn't bothered to check the viewer before opening it. "Can I help you with something, Miss Royal?"

Kelli extended her hand. "You can start by calling me Kelli." Her words sounded more like an entreaty than she had intended. He did not take her outstretched hand. She frowned, folded her arms, and continued in a more reserved tone. "This feels familiar — as a matter of fact, it's why I'm here. We need to talk."

Duncan's powerful frame blocked the doorway. His frosty

stare dared her to come closer. Seconds ticked by like hours. A gust of icy rain blew across the doorway. Kelli shivered, pulling the rain shield tighter. Defeated by the weather and her obstinance, Duncan stepped back, but not before looking around. It dawned on Kelli then to question the appropriateness of a student visiting a professor in his private apartment. Duncan nodded and said, "Come in, Miss Royal... Kelli."

"Thanks," Kelli mumbled, edging past him into the warmth of the apartment. Removing the ineffective rain shield, she moved toward the warmth of the fireplace. She stood with her back to Duncan, warming her hands. "What is it with you?" she asked. "Do you have a problem with me?"

"You're not who you appear to be, or say you are." His eyes closed in concentration. "Why aren't you using your actual name?" The tone of his voice dared Kelli to deny the accusation.

Startled, Kelli's stepped back, almost bumping into him. She turned, looking up at his face. It was a handsome face, a mixture of his European and Maori heritage clear in the powerful lines, dark curly hair, and almost golden eyes. "Is that what's bothering you?"

Those eyes met hers, demanding answers. "I've always sensed you were hiding something. Dr. Granger would never have considered a transfer student for this project. I don't trust liars, Miss Royal, and I know you're not who you say you are."

"I see what you mean," she replied. Dr. Granger had insisted that Kelli's identity should remain a secret from the students to protect the project, but it had been her decision to keep Duncan Meddars in the dark. Turning her face away from him, she reached up and popped out the green tinted contacts she was wearing. "My name is Kelli Leigh." She looked into his eyes, watching for his reaction. "I'd rather not explain my need for anonymity."

"Sweet Jesus, you're real," Duncan exclaimed, stepping back. "I never put much credence in those stories. The tabloids made it so sensational." He reached out and took her face in one of his firm hands without asking, tilting it up toward the light, searching for visible evidence of her unique genetic heritage. He said, "You don't look like the tabloid pictures. Are you an enhanced human?"

"No, I'm not an enhanced human. I had an excellent plastic surgeon. I'm half human. I think my father may have been Aldebarian." Kelli smiled self-consciously, pleased that his face had shown no revulsion. His hand still cupped her face.

"Does Dr. Granger know who you are?" Duncan asked, his voice a whisper.

"Of course, Dr. Granger and Michael both know." Kelli shifted defensively, freeing her face from his grasp. She had come here to confront Duncan, not give away her secrets. "They've known me since I was a student here at Barringer's," she continued. "They trust me. I hope you will too."

Kelli placed the contacts lenses in their small plastic case and slipped it into her pocket.

Duncan walked over to a small bar. "Would you like a drink?" he asked. "I know I could use one." Her gaze followed him, her body rigid. Duncan looked back at her and said, "Relax, I will not turn you in."

Relieved, Kelli turned back toward the fire. An actual fire in a fireplace was rare because wood was a precious commodity these days. The flames crackled and sparked, creating a frenzied dance as they gave up their energy. She watched for a moment, mesmerized by the leaping flames, then asked, "Do you have any coffee?"

Duncan rummaged in the kitchen. He emerged a few minutes later with two cups and a steaming pot. "I don't have coffee, but this is an excellent tea." He set the tray down and with surprising delicacy poured her a cup.

"Thanks." Kelli savored the spicy aroma before tasting. "Mmm. It's good, spicy-sweet like the smell," she remarked appreciatively.

Duncan nodded toward the sofa and said, "Please have a seat." He plopped on one end of the sofa, balancing a cup and saucer on his knee. Kelli took a seat at the other end, leaving an awkward space in the middle. Soon the warmth and intimacy of the fire eased the tension between them.

Duncan studied her tense posture and commented, "You should ditch the contacts. Your eyes are incredible."

"Michael says I am excessively paranoid." Kelli laughed, fidgeting with the lens case in her pocket. She sat the small plastic container on the coffee table and admitted, "I guess they could go."

"Agreed." Duncan scooped up the container and pitched it into the center of the fire.

Kelli jumped to retrieve the contacts, stopping short of plunging her hands into the flames. Her eyes widened in disbelief as she watched the plastic sizzle and melt. Her once tight control crumbled. "You…," she sputtered, fighting between anger and laughter.

"Arrogant Aussie?" Duncan supplied with a mischievous grin.

"You had no right. How am I supposed to explain a new eye color?" Kelli demanded with an amused glint in her eye. "The other students will notice if I walk in like this."

"Tell them you had your irises tinted—it's a popular procedure," Duncan countered diffidently, moving closer to refill her teacup. "What is that exotic fragrance you're wearing?"

Bewildered, Kelli replied, "I don't wear perfume, it gives me a rash."

"You're joking." Duncan grabbed her arm and sniffed several areas from the hand to the elbow. "That scent is definitely coming from your skin. Do you use scented soap or lotion?" he asked. Puzzled, Kelli shook her head. Duncan unceremoniously tested the other arm. Their eyes met, the fire reflecting purple flames in hers. The aroma grew more intense.

Kelli wasn't empathic, but she recognized the ardor in his eyes. It sent shivers of fear and self-revulsion coursing inside her. She was his student, for God's sake. She scooted back to the other end of the couch, putting a safer distance between them. It wasn't as if Kelli didn't find Duncan attractive; she did. The difference in their ages was less than three years, but his position as her teacher would make a romance impossible. Also, her traumatic experiences had taught her one thing; he was human, and she was not. She was an alien of undetermined origin. Dr. Poe had burned the despised phrase into her psyche.

Resolutely, she reminded herself there was no room in her life for romantic distractions. Kelli crossed her legs and looked purposefully at the clock.

"I'm sorry. That wasn't like me. I don't make passes at guests no matter how attractive they are." Duncan glanced at her rigid posture. "What time are we scheduled for immune booster therapy at the clinic tomorrow?"

"I won't be able to go. There is a lot of work I need to do," Kelli said.

Duncan turned his head and spoke reassuringly. "We're getting immunizations and immune boosters. It won't hurt a bit."

Kelli glared at him. "I know, but I would rather not." Her voice came out little more than a squeak. The fear was raw and overwhelming. The silence widened, and she retreated behind a calm veneer.

Her attention drifted to the window. The rain was letting up. Kelli needed to get away from Duncan's probing, and any reminder of the imminent clinic visit. Her anxiety increased. She experienced the rapid heart rate and mounting panic that preceded an episode. She struggled to control the flashback she felt coming on.

"The rain is stopping. I'll go before it starts again."

Kelli rose to her feet to say goodbye. Her progress with

Duncan was a good sign. The misting rain cooled her emotions as she walked home. The encounter had left her exhausted. Once inside her apartment, she swallowed a mild sedative before flopping across her bed.

CHAPTER EIGHT
—ALDEBAR PRIME—DEGG HOMELAND
People of Three

Shual moved down the corridor, the sound of his footsteps almost impossible to hear. This was his second time inside the Deggarian Capital Building. The attention he had received since finding the spy program was affecting his duties as senior programmer. The reports Rom Nebbar demanded seemed endless, and now he had summoned Shual to another briefing, this one before the high lord of Deggar, a personage of such importance that one never spoke his name.

Shual entered the chambers of the high lord. He stopped short as he realized that his host had another visitor. Shual had been told that the high lord was waiting for him, but not that he was entertaining an important guest. "My pardon. Lord, this one did not realize you had a guest."

"We need you here." The high lord stretched out a silvery hand, motioning Shual to come meet his visitor. "I believe you know Lord Ravon of Shamar. He is acting as the liaison with Earth."

Shual bowed in greeting. One admired the winged Shamaru people. They were noble, if sometimes arrogant and uneven-tempered. During the dark years of the Great Wars, the

Shamaru had protected the Degg homeland.

"My congratulations, Lord Ravon." Shual extended his hands with palms up, a gesture of peace and respect. He considered Lord Ravon a friend. For three years, they had attended school in Rishal together. It was common knowledge that Lord Travalla had handpicked Ravon to follow him as the high lord of Shamar.

Ravon returned his greeting and Shual took a seat on the floor before the two lords.

***

Lord Ravon was happy to see Shual again, but he had little use for Degg ceremony and protocol. He wanted to clasp Shual's arm in friendship, but that would have been much too familiar for a Degg. He maintained eye contact long enough to let Shual know he recognized him. "What have you learned about the information leak?"

"The alien program apparently attached to our communications network. How it could access our transmission from Earth is still a mystery. I've traced the source to Earth, but not to the UNWL. In fact, it duplicates most of the information that was already provided to the Earth government."

Rom Eutte, the high lord of Deggar's voice was quiet, thoughtful. "Could they be confirming the information, making sure our reports are accurate?"

"Possibly, but I've examined the UNWL transmission packet. Its technology is inferior." Shual had spent the last Aldebarian week trying to trace it backwards from the Aldebarian network to the Earth transmission without destroying either of them. "We cannot break the link it has with our network."

"You have our permission to dispose of it." Rom Eutte made a face. "One hates dealing with distasteful matters. However, one faces reality, and the need for security officers and powerful friends."

"One does not advise that, my lord," Shual began, and was most relieved that Eutte took no offense at his liberty.

"I have noted your advice, Senior Programmer. Do you know more than you have shared? Lord Ravon may hear everything. He oversees relations between Earth and Aldebar." The high lord nodded to Shual. "You may continue."

"Thank you, my lord. Someone monitoring the Earth government, not us, sent the link. If we destroy the program, we break that link, and alert whoever is responsible for its presence. One can analyze it from this end and feed it information. We will eventually locate its source," Shual said, and added, "This one hopes he was not overstepping his place by expressing his ability in this matter."

"You have our permission to proceed with this plan," Eutte answered. He added with deference, "We appreciate your wisdom in this matter."

Shual flushed darkest silver at such praise.

***

Lord Ravon hailed Shual on the way out of the capital building. He wasn't sure if it would flatter or offend a Degg to be singled out publicly, but he wanted to speak with him.

"Greetings, my lord Ravon," Shual responded in the respectful tone of his people.

"Greetings, friend. Have they made you Rom yet?" Ravon caught up with Shual and they walked in step outside. Ravon donned a shield against the bright sun and dry sandy air. At least it wasn't the season for sandstorms.

Shual shook his head and replied in his most scholarly tone. "They do not make one a Rom, friend Ravon. It is a title of respect that is earned by much diligence and service. You should remember that from your years in Rishal."

"Of course, friend Shual," Ravon answered, and tried to remember what he had learned of the Degg. They were a strange lot, and very formal. He knew it would not be appropriate to ask about Shual's family—that would be much too familiar. The male Degg and the small willowy female Degg seldom left the homeland of Deggar. The asexual worker Degg were taller and more intelligent than either of the parenting Degg. Shual was a worker Degg. Though he would never marry or produce offspring, he could hold many jobs and rise to the level of Rom, or even higher. The high lord of Deggar was always a worker Degg, as befitted one whose life was one of service to his people. That was it. That was all he knew.

"I brought you something from Shamar," Lord Ravon said, tossing a small bag to Shual. It contained a rare pink stone, the stone of memories. "Lady Travalla tells me this stone enables its bearer to recall experiences. I hope you will use it to recall our friendship and my admiration for your people."

Shual's mouth opened and his lips rippled as he let out a gasp. "This one is most honored by your gift. It is a rare stone indeed. Had I purchased it on the market, it would have cost many months' salary."

Ravon was pleased his gift seemed to thrill Shual. He was also pleased to be working with someone he could trust.

"You must join me for a meal and meet this one's family," Shual said.

Ravon was so surprised that he stumbled and had to catch himself. The Degg were a very private people, and outsiders rarely met parenting Degg. "It is too great an honor, friend."

Shual bounced like a child expecting a treat, and a soft musical hum vibrated from his body. "No, the honor is ours, Lord Ravon. One of my younger siblings is also a worker, and soon to enter the open school in Rishal. He would love to meet you."

"Then I will accept and apologize in advance for my vulgar lack of knowledge and manners," Ravon answered.

"Yes, very well spoken. That sounded almost like it came from a Degg," Shual said. "It is not far across the sands to the nesting home of this one. We will be there in an hour, and back before dark."

Ravon flexed his wings. It would be quicker to fly, but not safe. The sand-filled winds of the desert would sting his eyes and damage his flight feathers. Those would take weeks to heal.

They boarded a glass enclosed bus that would stop in the tiny village where Shual's family lived. Ravon was the only Shamaru on the bus. He was almost sure that no Shamaru had ever ridden on the bus before. The other passengers nodded as Ravon made his way down the aisle. Their mouths rippled in surprise, but they quickly lowered their gazes. Ravon thought he detected a hint of smugness and pride in Shual's walk. He bit back a smile. *That would be unbecoming in a Degg, so I must be wrong.*

The wind had picked up when they departed the bus. Shual handed him a mask and a clear visor. Ravon was grateful for both. Ravon shook his wings to get the sand off, but it was of little use. It would take a thorough cleaning to make the tiny grains dislodge. He would not offend his friend by complaining.

He followed Shual down a paved street covered with sand. Shual stopped in front of what looked like a giant bowl turned upside down next to the street. Shual clapped his hands and sang a greeting in the Degg language. Soon a door opened and Ravon realized that this was the top half of a large home. The other half burrowed under the sand.

Shual's parents greeted them. Ravon had been told that worker Degg were larger than parenting Degg, but he hadn't expected Shual to tower a good eight inches above his parents.

"Come inside," said Shual's father.

They went inside and the air was cool. Ravon wanted to spread out his wings and shake and shake until the sand fell to the floor. The diminutive female Degg seemed to read his mind. She turned to Shual and said something Ravon didn't understand.

Shual translated. "My mother says we are to go to the wind baths. She has no clothes large enough for you, but yours will air out in the bath. If we hurry, we can get clean before the meal."

Ravon followed Shual to the far end of the house. A blue marble door opened at Shual's touch. Inside, marble tiles covered with images of birds and trees lined the walls. The floor was a fine mesh of silver metal fitted like a sieve over a square pit.

"Take off your shoes," said Shual as he unfastened his own and tossed them in the hall. "First, we will have our feet washed."

Ravon, who had paid an extravagant price for his shoes, did so. The door closed and Shual motioned for him to step out onto the silver metal. There was a sound of humming as soft sprays of water cleansed his feet. It massaged and warmed him, but did not go above his ankles. Next, warm jets of air dried his feet and eased the tension in his legs.

Shual was clearly enjoying the bath. "Hold out your arms and extend your wings." He moved over to give Ravon room.

The air whirled around him like a small gentle cyclone, lifting the dirt and sand from his body and wings. His robes billowed around him, becoming fresh and wrinkle free. The air lifted sand and dirt into the grates at the top of the room. When it stopped, Ravon sighed. He almost didn't need a comb for his wings. Each feather had fallen into place.

"Hurry or we will be late."

Shual's family waited, seated on pillows around a low stone table. Ravon had to pull in and fold his wings. Several Degg children, small and delicate, watched him with large slitted eyes. The brother who would follow Shual as a worker Degg sat a little apart, already larger than the parents.

They passed around an enormous platter with steaks cut from a giant sand worm, followed by smaller trays of cactus, boiled lizard eggs, and bread. Even the children drank the wine that was served with the meal. Shual explained that in Deggar water was precious, and always treated with chemicals before it was safe to drink.

"Is it true there will be an exchange of students with Earth, and they will come to Rishal?" asked Rathio, Shual's brother.

"Forgive his rudeness, Lord Ravon," said their mother. This one spends all his time on information sources and rumors. He must learn to hold his unseemly tongue so he does not shame us."

Rathio lowered his head.

"Your son gave no offense," said Ravon. "Arrangements are being made now for the student exchange."

Rathio looked up, a dark expression on his face. "I have heard that there will also be Narr students for the first time in Rishal's open school."

A look of surprise and concern crossed Shual's face. Ravon nodded, confirming the news. It troubled him that the Narr would send students after so long a time, but it was not unexpected.

CHAPTER NINE
—EARTH—BARRINGER'S INSTITUTE
A Man Who Sees

Duncan watched as Kelli boarded the shuttle bus ahead of him to go to the clinic. She swatted her left temple as if trying to clear her ear. Her lips were parted as she seemed to breathe in quick gasps through her mouth. A wave of smothering fear washed over him as he tried to reach her telepathically. He boarded and took a seat a couple of rows behind her. There was no reason to be afraid — there would be no need for genetic tests, and no one was going to hold her against her will. Still, he felt the panic wrenching her empty stomach. Flashbacks? He could feel her fighting them. She had not confided in Michael or Dr. Granger about the existence of flashbacks. That would have raised doubts about her mental stability. Did she not trust them or him with all her secrets?

He saw her look around and relax a little. She was watching Michael talking to redheaded Niles Webster, excitement and adventure shining in their eyes. Niles had become Michael's shadow since being selected for the Aldebar team. He was gesturing as he chattered to Michael. They seemed caught up in an intense conversation, unaware of Kelli and the tide of fear engulfing her. *Bind Niles' hands and he would be unable to speak,*

Duncan thought. This brought a smile and eased his own nerves a little.

Stepping down from the bus behind Kelli, Duncan sensed her trepidation, noticing a slight jitteriness in her graceful movements. He caught up and whispered, "Are you okay?" as they entered the clinic.

"I'm fine," Kelli snapped.

Duncan looked pointedly down at her shaking hands and frowned. She didn't want him drawing attention to the fact that she was falling apart. She turned and walked ahead.

Michael handed the list of team members to the medical receptionist. The next few minutes passed in a blur. Duncan never took his eyes off Kelli.

"Kelli Royal? Please follow me." The prim, white-clad nurse pointed down a hallway lined with exam rooms. Kelli swayed, then turned as if to run for the nearest exit. The nurse looked back over her shoulder at Kelli's pale face. She asked, "Miss Royal, are you all right?" Kelli's lips moved as if to answer, but the door cut off her reply as it closed.

Duncan heard the nurse's distress call and saw an intern running in to answer. In unison, he and Michael followed. They found Kelli curled in a fetal ball on the floor, shaking. She was in the throes of a flashback, her head tossing back and forth as her body convulsed. Kelli's lips moved silently, begging the ghost doctors to stop hurting her.

The young clinic doctor went to work, checking her vital signs and putting a pillow under her head. "She's having a seizure. We'll move her into one of the other rooms and sedate her for now," he said. He directed the nurse to call for an ambulance. "They'll take her straight to the medical center downtown," he explained.

The receptionist shoved release papers at Michael. Duncan peered warily over Michael's shoulder, scanning the forms. As Kelli's "supervisor," Michael could allow the medical treatments.

He was on the verge of signing the forms when Duncan discretely tried to get his attention by coughing. Michael didn't notice subtlety, so Duncan roughly grabbed the pen from his hand. Michael's fist clenched, automatically drawing back. He checked the swing. "What are you doing?" he demanded of Duncan.

"Sign nothing," Duncan warned. "Let's get her out of here."

"Why? She needs medical attention," said Michael.

"She's having flashbacks," Duncan answered. "Her emotions were overpowering as soon as we rushed in the room." This was a recent phenomenon for Duncan, though he understood it was a commonplace occurrence among empaths. He looked at Michael and continued. "Something about this place caused them. We need to take her back to the campus."

"Are you sure?" Michael looked at Kelli lying helplessly on the floor. There was conviction in Duncan's voice. A clinic doctor returned to supervise Kelli's transfer and sedation. Bending, Michael lifted Kelli into his arms, knocking the doctor aside. He handed her to Duncan. "Take her back to Barringer's and have Dr. Granger look at her. If she doesn't come around soon, get her to a hospital."

"Stop! Don't move her until an ambulance arrives," the angry doctor shouted as he jumped to his feet. "She needs medical attention."

Michael blocked the doctor's path, allowing Duncan to escape the room. Duncan pushed past nurses and concerned students, carrying Kelli in his arms. She was light, unexpectedly light. She couldn't weigh over ninety pounds, and that was a generous estimate. He couldn't explain it. Kelli was slim, but she was a tall woman and not fashion-model thin. Could her bones be that lite? Were they hollow? Ignoring repeated calls to stop, Duncan strained the muscles in his powerful legs, charging at full speed toward the exit.

Outside, the chilly wind stung Duncan's face. Somewhere,

in the back of his mind, he remembered his new leather jacket hanging in the waiting area of the clinic. He wished he had it on. Kelli's shaking had subsided into gentle sobs. "That's right, cry it out, little Sheila." Duncan shifted her in his arms so her head rested more on his shoulder for support. He looked around the parking lot, trying to determine the best course of action. Hailing an air-cab with an unconscious woman in his arms would be next to impossible. He looked down the street toward a shuttle stop and started walking again. He would figure out his next move once they made it that far.

A dissonant blare from the road caught his attention. "Over here, Dr. Meddars, get in. Security will be here soon," a deep voice called from the passenger side of a flashy auto-jet. A man was leaning his body halfway out the window, waving at them. An older woman wearing a dark scarf was driving. Duncan jerked open the door and pushed Kelli's limp body in and then followed.

He settled into the cramped backseat, cradling Kelli in his arms. Once or twice during the quick ride back to Barringer's, he thought she murmured someone's name. *Who is Eric?*

"It's okay, Princess, the programming worked." The man leaned over the seat and patted Kelli's hand.

So, this is Eric, Duncan thought. By the time they reached Barringer's, Kelli had fallen into a fretful sleep. The man called Eric jumped out and ran ahead toward the administration building. Duncan gently lifted Kelli and followed at a gentle pace.

Dr. Granger met them at the door, leading them to his office. Duncan looked around for the man called Eric, but he had disappeared as quickly as he arrived. "Put her down over here," Dr. Granger said, pointing toward the ivory divan. "What happened?"

Duncan lowered Kelli and flexed the aching muscles in his shoulder. He said, "On the way to the clinic she seemed very tense. I don't know what happened in the exam room, but I think

she's having flashbacks, reliving some traumatic experience."
Duncan had never had an empathic episode. He fought to keep
the sensations from overwhelming his emotions. He could
understand why many empaths cursed their gift.

"That's likely," Dr. Granger nodded. He took out a small
flashlight and checked the response of Kelli's pupils. "How well
do you know Kelli?"

Duncan didn't miss the underlying question. "I know
she's Kelli Leigh," he answered.

"Are you familiar with post-traumatic stress disorder?
They held this girl at a U.N.W.L. clinic for several months. I
don't know all the details, but it's fair to say they subjected her to
repeated physical and mental abuse."

Duncan's voice was heavy with sadness. "What did they
do to her?"

"God only knows; everything short of an autopsy." Dr.
Granger shook his head. "The details would make a long, rather
painful story, and I need to bring her around now," he continued.
"She may explain what happened at the clinic."

"Will this help?" Margaret had slipped in. She handed Dr.
Granger a wet hand towel. He wiped it across Kelli's forehead.
Duncan rubbed her hands in his, whispering her name. He
looked at Mrs. Ashford. She nodded in response to Duncan's
silent inquiry. She understood what was happening.

Kelli responded to Duncan's voice. Her mind cleared
slowly, as if she were waking from a deep sleep. She glanced
around Dr. Granger's office, trying to remember where she
was, and rubbed her face. It felt damp from tears. She looked at
Duncan, wanting to ask how badly she had freaked out in the
clinic.

"Are you feeling better, kid?" Duncan asked. The color
was coming back into Kelli's face. Her breathing had settled into
its natural rhythm.

"You brought me out of the clinic," she said groggily, "I

remember a sensation of being carried and your voice. Were you talking to Eric?"

Margaret put a delicate hand firmly on Duncan's shoulder. "Give her a little time to rest," she said. "Dr. Gentry called from the clinic. You can take it at my desk."

***

Duncan was sitting at Kelli's side. On the phone, Professor Gentry had been in a rare temper. Kelli squeezed Duncan's hand in appreciation, but nodded toward the door. Duncan shook hands with Michael and slipped out, giving them privacy.

Kelli had been mentally berating herself for over an hour when Michael arrived. She expected and deserved his anger. Before he could speak, she said, "I'm an idiot. The entire project is in danger because I was too proud to admit the flashbacks were a problem."

Michael put an arm around Kelli's shoulder and asked, "Want to talk about what happened?"

"I'm so sorry, Michael. I should have warned you about the flashbacks. I thought I could control them." Her voice was shaky. "I haven't had one in months." There was nowhere to look except in Michael's eyes. They held forgiveness and understanding. Kelli wasn't ready to forgive herself. His gentleness and concern brought tears to her eyes.

"It's over now," Michael said, stroking the back of her neck. "The clinic is sending someone out tomorrow to give you the immunizations. Can you talk about the flashbacks?"

"I can't," Kelli tried to explain. "I remember being terrified, lots of pain, but that's all. I wish I could tell you more. What did you tell the students?"

"That you had an allergic reaction to something you ate for breakfast and had a seizure." Michael had stuck as close to the truth as possible. "Dr. Granger wants to treat you with a reality visor. He thinks he can help you control the flashbacks."

"He does? That would be great," Kelli said with relief.

"I said control, not cure, but yes, he thinks he can help." Michael stroked her hair. "You and Duncan seem to have patched up your differences."

"I went over to have it out with him and wound up telling him the truth." Kelli warmed up to the topic, unaware that Michael was referring to the intimate tête-à-tête he had observed and Duncan's protectiveness. "He's nice, for a conceited Aussie."

"You're looking better," Margaret said from the doorway, giving Kelli a smile. She gave Professor Gentry a cool look. "You're not giving the poor girl one of your lectures, are you? Don't make her feel any worse. Rest and some hot tea are what she needs."

"After your instructions, Margaret, I wouldn't dare," he replied

Kelli laughed and took Michael's hand to steady herself. She stood and said, "I'm feeling much better, Margaret. In fact, I wouldn't mind having lunch. I'm starved."

CHAPTER TEN
—ALDEBAR PRIME—SHAMARU HOMELAND

A kick to the abdomen sent Lord Ravon flying, gasping for breath. His wings beat furiously to keep him aloft. He responded with a volley of ferocious blows that sent his sparring partner crashing into the side of the cliff. Bennia raised his hands in surrender.

"Peace, Adomi, this is not a death battle. Cool your anger, my lord."

Ravon stopped and hung in the air, his breath coming in gasps. Forcing down his anger, he nodded.

"I take it your appearance today did not go well. Want to talk about it?" Bennia pointed to a natural ledge on the mountain not far away. "I would find it preferable to having my neck broken."

Ravon sat cross-legged on the ledge and lowered his head into his hands. "They've dogged my meetings for weeks. I looked like an utter fool. They knew things that haven't been released publicly. They opposed every decision I've made about the student exchange, and constantly brought up my age and lack of experience."

"You have the full support of Lord Travalla and most of the council," Bennia said. "Have you wondered if a spy is giving someone confidential information to discredit you and sabotage the exchange? Not everyone supports welcoming these humans to Aldebar."

"You echo my fears. I have tried to assure everyone that it is safe for the students to come here, and for our students to visit Earth."

"Any idea who is behind the lies circulating throughout the homelands?" Bennia asked. He was Lord Ravon's lifelong friend and sparring partner. They kept no secrets from each other, and worked out together as often as their busy schedules allowed.

"If I had any idea, I'd be ripping their heads off instead of sitting around looking like an idiot," Ravon answered. "We're doing a security sweep. Someone must know my schedule and have access to my personal files to orchestrate this. I've called in a Deggarian expert to run a check. In fact, the high lord of Deggar has assigned Shual to the project."

"A Degg?" said Bennia.

"Rema Shual is one of the brightest and most honorable men I know," said Ravon. "I trust him completely."

"All Degg are honorable. Ask one, he'll tell you it's an inbred quality, common to their species." Bennia laughed. He knocked Ravon off the ledge and the sparring bout resumed.

They finished the match and Ravon had just stepped out of a shower when a voice hailed him. "Hold on, I'm coming," he answered.

The expression on the face of Lord Travalla's aide did not bode well. Ravon motioned for him to come in. Pillot was a security officer assigned to help Shual track down the source of the leak to the radicals.

"You've found a name?" Ravon's tone made the words more of a statement than a question.

The aide nodded. "Lord Rischar." Disgust and disbelief were palpable in the words. "How do I tell my lord that one of his own kin has betrayed him?"

Lord Ravon shook his head. He had feared as much. "I'll break the news. It won't surprise him. He has little love for Rischar."

"No, it was my assignment, and I'll tell him." The aide placed a hand on Ravon's shoulder. "I thank the spirit of our ancestors every day that he has you."

The praise heartened Ravon, and knowing who was behind the attacks restored his self-confidence. There were ways to deal with traitors and spies. He would turn the tables on Rischar. He debated several strategies, but decided the best course was not to let Rischar know he had discovered his treachery. *We can then feed him false information.*

CHAPTER ELEVEN
—Earth—Barringer's Institute

Two weeks had passed since Kelli's abysmal failure at the clinic, her total meltdown. It had taken days before she could look at Michael Gentry without trying to apologize again. Sure, she had her immunizations at Barringer's the next day, but that didn't change the fact that she had a major flashback and wound up curled on the floor seizing. Duncan's quick actions to get her out of there had saved her from being back in UNWL custody, and the entire Aldebar Project from being scrapped. Eric was furious. Dr. Granger's idea was her only hope of controlling the flashbacks. She would have to take herself off the project. The thought of that brought a taste of bitter gall to her mouth.

She blinked. The dim lights muted the familiar furnishings in Dr. Granger's office and softened the age lines in his face. He held Kelli's shaking hands with his own, stilling their trembling. "This is a safe procedure. When you're ready, we'll begin the regression process."

"Are you sure you can bring me out of the flashback?" she asked.

"Yes, I can bring you out at any time. You'll be reliving the events, but it will be like watching a movie."

Kelli moistened her lips. The relaxant made her mouth dry

and cottony, but she could feel it softening the jittery sensations in her stomach. She could do this. She was warmed by a feeling of safety.

"Will I be aware of you?" she asked.

"You'll be able to hear my voice and talk to me," Dr. Granger explained. "It's very important for you to describe everything you see and feel."

Kelli squeezed Dr. Granger's hand and nodded toward the visor. He fitted the cap on her head and lowered the visor over her eyes. Giving her shoulder a pat, he activated the VR visor. A soft humming sound filled the room. She smiled as light came from the visor, pulsing to the rhythm of the humming. The rhythm increased, the tempo pulsing in her head.

In seconds, she was slipping away in the whirling lights. After a few minutes, she couldn't feel the chair she was in or Dr. Granger's touch. The sound and the lights were real, nothing else. As the sound softened, the lights dimmed and her eyes focused. Her vision cleared. Someone was crying, and Kelli realized with a start that she was hearing herself. She looked around and recognized her room at Poe's clinic. She turned toward the crying and saw herself as she had been at thirteen, huddled in the corner sobbing.

"Oh, God," she gasped.

"Kelli, talk to me." Dr. Granger's calm voice seemed to emanate from another dimension, "Tell me what you see."

"It's me," said Kelli. "I can see myself. This is weird."

"Relax," Dr. Granger's voice commanded. "Tell me where you are and what's happening."

Kelli felt him tighten his grasp on her hand. It reassured her, despite her virtual surroundings. She smiled.

He asked, "Did you feel that? I'm right here. I won't leave you, just keep talking."

Heartened by his words, Kelli described what she was experiencing. "I'm at Poe's clinic in a small basement room."

"What's happening?"

"I'm crying for my mother," Kelli continued. "They brought me to the center two months ago and I haven't seen her. I'm so scared." She paused a moment, then went on. "Dr. Poe is coming back. I can hear him in the hall. They won't leave me alone. They keep asking the same questions and doing tests. The tests hurt. I have needle tracks on both arms. I overheard them talking earlier, Dr. Poe wants to remove some eggs from my ovaries and see if he can fertilize them."

Kelli's agitation increased. Her voice tensed and grew high pitched. "They're in the room now. I'm trying to get away. I'm not strong, but I leave a long scratch on his face. My screams are deafening. They're giving me a shot to make me sleep. It's over now; they carried me to the operating room."

"Okay, we are going to move ahead now." Dr. Granger's voice returned to guide her. "It's two weeks later. What's happening?"

For a few moments, the lights and humming sound returned, then Kelli found herself in a small hospital room. There she could see a young, ill looking girl sleeping, an I.V. bag attached to her arm. A guard sat by the door reading. Kelli recognized herself. She remembered and reported, "I'm in the hospital. Dr. Poe is angry because I won't eat. I'm too tired to eat. He says my mother signed consent forms for the tests, but I don't believe him. She would never hurt me. I want to go home. I want my mother."

Dr. Granger's voice urged her, "Go on to the next day."

Kelli responded, "I'm in a room with Dr. Poe and several nurses. They finished doing a neuro-scan, testing my brain wave patterns. It didn't hurt, and I'm not all woozy from medication. They're setting up another test. No, stop. They're using an electric shock. It hurts! It hurts!"

Doctor Granger's response was commanding. "Kelli, relax and breathe. Remember, you're running a program. Try to distance your emotions. Let's see the end of your captivity. It is almost December. Find the last week you were there."

Lights and sounds whirled, but nothing appeared. Kelli felt a chill of fear engulf her. There was something here she didn't want to see, though she knew Eric and Michael would soon come to rescue her. She shook her head in frustration. "I can't see anything. I can't get past the fear."

His voice replied, "I'm increasing the frequency of the visor. I want you to concentrate and try to remember."

The darkness disappeared. There was venom in Kelli's voice as she described the scene. "There's a man in the waiting room," she said. "He is a UNWL security agent, not a doctor. He's been interrogating me for over an hour, asking the same questions over and over. I tell him I know no more about my father. He calls me a liar, then slaps me, hard. He laughs at my tears and tells me I'm never going to see my mother again, that she doesn't want an alien monster's child."

The concerned voice of Dr. Granger broke in, warning her. "Your pulse is too fast, Kelli. Take a breath and distance yourself from the emotions. We know he was filling your mind with lies. They locked your mother up for not cooperating with the government investigation. She searched for you when she got out." Outrage was clear in the vehemence with which he repudiated what she had been told.

Kelli pushed back her anger. In the interrogation's aftermath, she watched the young Kelli curl up in a tight ball and cry herself to sleep. It was a sight she couldn't describe to Dr. Granger. She yearned to reach out and comfort her younger self. If Eric hadn't found her message in the game and contacted Professor Gentry, she would have found some way to take her own life.

Dr. Granger instructed her to go to the day she escaped. "I fought them as much as I could, but it was no use. Poe won, and I am lying strapped down to the bed. They shaved my head, and they hooked IVs and machines up to me. I can't wake up. Professor Gentry enters the room and I can't respond. They're getting me out. It's over."

Dr. Granger said, "Yes, it is over, and you are safe. I'm going to bring you out of the program now. You've faced the memories, and you won. You won back then, too. Dr. Poe is dead, and he can't hurt you anymore. It's all behind you." He eased Kelli back from the program, reading encouragement from a prepared script in one of the books on reality therapy. When he was sure that she had returned to the present and was aware of her surroundings, he removed the visor and cap.

Dr. Granger mopped his face with a starched white handkerchief. With her hair loose and tousled, Kelli could have been mistaken for a much younger girl. He stroked her hair and planted a kiss on top of her head. "My dear brave child, I hope you find what you are looking for."

"It's there, I know it's there," Kelli answered, smiling up at the portly old gentleman. The bushy gray eyebrows almost hid his bright blue eyes. "Are those tears I see?" Kelli reached up and kissed his leathery cheek. "I'll miss you, you old softy," she whispered.

"Nonsense," he assured her. "You'll be much too busy living the adventure to think about me." Dr. Granger straightened his jacket and tried to regain his composure. "You should lie back and rest for a little while now. Go to sleep if you can."

Kelli woke three hours later. She stretched to relieve the stiffness in her back and looked at her clock. If she didn't hurry, she would be late. She was having lunch with one of her friends. Tracy had sounded upset when she called earlier. Team training would begin in three days, and there was no time to reflect on her therapy session. Every day, it seemed like a fresh crisis would threaten the project.

***

Tracy sat at a table in the school cafeteria, staring at a

soy burger and salad. She looked like she had been crying. Kelli grabbed a salad from the line and joined her. "Sorry I'm late. My meeting with Dr. Granger took longer than I expected."

"Oh, that's all right," Tracy responded in a subdued voice. Something had dampened her bubbly personality. "Do you want the bad news now or after you eat?"

"Give it to me now."

"How would you feel if I didn't go to Aldebar?" Tracy asked. "I know I promised we could be roomies, but I don't think I can go."

"I'm so sorry," Kelli said. She reached out and took Tracy's hand. "I've heard that your mother is in the hospital. Is that why you're staying here?"

Tracy nodded and replied, "I kept hoping she'd improve, but she isn't. The doctors don't think she'll be alive when I return." Tears welled up in her eyes. "Niles and I have been dating for over a year, and I hate letting him go without me, but I don't think my dad can handle this alone. He loves Mom so much. We both do." She swiped at the tracks running down her cheeks, smearing the carefully applied makeup.

"That's okay. I think you're doing the right thing," Kelli comforted. She felt for the bright seventeen-year-old. She would talk to Michael later; perhaps it wasn't too late to select an alternate.

"They'll need someone to take my place," Tracy said. "The alternates are both guys, and that doesn't seem fair. Ammie Franks has all the paperwork in and she's dying to go. Do you think you could talk to Dr. Granger and Professor Gentry for her?"

"Why me? I'm just another student."

"Dr, Granger likes you, everyone knows that. We think he'll listen to you."

On cue, Ammie Franks appeared at their table, her blonde curls framing her tiny oval face. She looked at Kelli with her large blue eyes.

Kelli shook her head and tried to convey her displeasure, though she admired the girl's determination. She explained, "Ammie has talked to Professor Gentry about this before. The Aldebar team is open to junior and senior students. The age requirement is sixteen. Ammie is fourteen. That may not seem fair, but not everything in life is fair."

Ammie pleaded, "I'm interested in the space program." Her French accent and a slight lisp added to her aura of sophistication. Ammie was flamboyant, but she was one of the brightest students at Barringer's, and mature for her age. She was also stubborn, and she had come prepared. "See, I have brought the court papers. I'm emancipated. In the eyes of the courts, I'm an adult."

Kelli looked at the papers and murmured, "I thought your uncle was your guardian."

"No, he acts as my business advisor," Ammie explained. "When Grand-meme died last year, I petitioned for emancipation and the courts granted me adult status."

Kelli continued to read the court papers. They verified Ammie's words. Whether it would be enough to convince Dr. Granger, Kelli didn't know. She hated to raise false hopes and disappoint Ammie again. "I can't give you an answer. I'll talk to Dr. Granger and Professor Gentry when Tracy cancels, but they'll make the final decision."

"Yes. Oh, thank you, Kelli. Thank you."

The team members debated Ammie's application later that evening in Dr. Granger's office. Kelli felt she should not take part in the discussion, since Ammie was a friend and she was partial to the young French girl.

"Nonsense, you know her better than any of us," Dr. Granger insisted. "I trust you can give an unbiased opinion."

"Well, Ammie is mature for her age," Kelli began. "But I don't think she comprehends the commitment. Three years is a lifetime for a fourteen-year-old. I don't know what would happen if she changed her mind after we launch, or if she can't handle the stress of living in an alien culture."

"I asked those same questions about myself," Duncan interjected. "Ammie has a genius IQ, and she's raised herself while running a multinational corporation."

"Could she fit into the team? How does she respond to authority?" Michael questioned.

"I don't know," said Kelli. "She's stubborn, independent, and impulsive, but she's determined to reach Aldebar."

Michael's face broke into an amused grin. Dr. Granger and Duncan shared the humor, and Duncan stifled a laugh.

"What's so funny?" Kelli demanded.

Dr. Granger patted Kelli's shoulder. "That description fits someone else we all know and love," he answered.

Feigning ignorance, Kelli passed out copies of the court documents, which granted Ammie adult status and would protect the school should problems occur.

Michael voted against Ammie. He stated, "I don't think we should bend the rules for one student. It's not fair to the others, and they might resent her."

"If those are your major objections, why not let the students decide?" Duncan suggested. "They can't accuse us of favoritism if they make the final decision."

Dr. Granger looked from Michael to Duncan, observing their interaction. He asked, "Can we agree then that, if the current exchange students are in favor of allowing Ammie to go, we'll honor that decision?"

The next day, they summoned the nine original exchange students for a meeting. Michael presented Ammie's situation, not showing the leadership's position.

Kelli kept a low profile during the meeting. She didn't meet Tracy's eyes. Niles Webster became the spokesperson for the students.

"We're honored you included us in this decision, and we want to be fair. Can we have time for deliberations?"

"Yes, of course. That's an excellent idea. Call me when you decide," Michael Gentry said, and left the students to their discussions.

After reviewing Ammie's file and the Aldebar Project's application procedure, they asked to see the court papers. They met for another hour. When they emerged, they had decided and elected Niles Webster to present the results to the professors.

Niles stood in front of Dr. Granger, Professor Gentry, and Duncan Meddars, shuffling Ammie's court papers as he reported. "We all like Ammie, and have wanted her on the team from the start. But in fairness to the other applicants, we had to justify making an exception for her. You dumped a hard problem in our laps. The pros and cons seemed to balance out, so we took a secret ballot. If everyone voted in favor of Ammie, she could go. If even one member voted no, she was out." Niles paused before concluding, "We want to congratulate her on being selected for the Aldebar Exchange Program."

Cheers went up from the other students, and Kelli contacted Ammie on the Visa-phone. Ammie rushed over and the evening became a celebration party. Pent up excitement and nerves carried them late into the evening. It was a time of team bonding and the leaders approved, though Dr. Granger turned in much earlier than the others.

CHAPTER TWELVE
—ALDEBAR PRIME—NARR REGION

Ubal leaned against the chair's special neck rest. He had brought in the only decent piece of furniture in the building because he wanted to at least sit back in comfort while he waited for his visitor to arrive. He smirked and imagined what the fastidious Shamaru, Lord Rischar, would think of the deserted building he had chosen for their first face-to-face meeting. It was in an isolated area of Hopisi, one of three cities in the Narr homeland open to outsiders. Most of his people shunned it, and it offered little to interest outsiders. The streets throughout the city were crumbling, full of potholes and missing street signs. The buildings were unpainted and in a state of disrepair. It was a haven for the worst criminals from the seven homelands. There were no police or security forces to hinder them.

Ubal smiled at the look of disgust on Lord Rischar's face as he entered. "Greetings, my lord Rischar. I trust your journey was pleasant," Ubal said. His words brought a scowl from his guest. Lord Rischar looked around before throwing off the robes covering his wings. While the young lord did not boast the famed Shamaru battle wings, his were impressive. A mixture of black, silver, and gray feathers in pristine condition, but a rather too short wingspan, Ubal decided.

"I was expecting Lord Gorron." Rischar raised an eyebrow. He stood looking at Ubal as if he expected the Narr to bow and clean off his boots.

Ubal's head bobbed as he tottered toward Lord Rischar. He pointed toward a chair. He suppressed a laugh as the Shamaru dusted the chair before sitting down.

"Lord Goron's presence would put you in danger," Ubal said. "Many are aware of our opposition to Lord Travalla."

Lord Rischar nodded. "I have tried to persuade him to step down from the council."

"We hear that Lord Ravon is to be his heir. That would not please the Narr alliance." Ubal studied the Shamaru's reaction. It showed anger, but not surprise. "Lord Gorron feels you would be a much better choice. Your leadership would provide the true unity the council needs."

The Shamaru puffed with self-importance. Ubal thought he might preen his feathers. "My uncle is old and cannot see anyone else's point of view. He has become a liability to the council."

Long tapering fingers waved as if shooing flies. "He won't live forever. Lord Ravon is our real problem," Ubal ventured.

"Yes, an even bigger fool. He would make things worse, not better." Lord Rischar's voice rose in anger. He was falling right in with Ubal's plan — or more, Lord Gorron's plans.

"That is why Lord Gorron arranged this meeting. You can help to discredit Lord Ravon. The council is giving away our technology to the humans. The exchange program must fail."

Lord Rischar nodded in agreement. "How can we accomplish that?"

Ubal let out his breath in what for a Narr was a sigh. He knew it sounded more like a serpent's hiss to the Shamaru, so he smiled and tottered to his seat. Ubal had purchased the computer virus at great expense, and had it programmed by an expert. Lord Gorron was not yet aware of how much Ubal had spent on the virus, but it would be worth it if the plan worked. Lord Ravon's change of plans made Lord Rischar crucial to the success of Ubal's master. If it didn't work, both Ubal and this Shamaru traitor would pay the price with their lives.

"Lord Ravon oversees the exchange between Aldebar and Earth. If that exchange were to fail, public sentiment would turn against Ravon and his sponsor, Lord Travalla." Ubal guarded his words. He watched Lord Rischar. If the Shamaru showed any signs of reluctance, he would drop the negotiations and come up with an alternate plan. Lord Rischar looked eager.

Ubal slid a small envelope out of the pocket of his robe. "This will introduce a virus in the Earth network. It will damage their shuttle and negotiations between the worlds will crumble."

At first Lord Rischar frowned, then his face brightened. "That would discredit Lord Ravon, and Travalla will have to withdraw his support. If he doesn't, Travalla could lose his position as head of the Council of Unity."

Ubal nodded in satisfaction. Rischar had come to the desired conclusion. "The Narr will support you as an alternate to Travalla's leadership. Lord Gorron does not object to the Shamaru maintaining the leadership of the council."

A look of utter disbelief crossed the Shamaru's face. He smiled. Ubal nodded in confirmation. He showed the small package and held it out. After a moment of hesitation, Lord Rischar took it.

"There must be nothing linking the Narr to this. Inside, you will find a name and location in the Bengari homeland. Deliver this message and you will have proven yourself to Lord Gorron and will have his complete support," Ubal began. He noted concern and reassured Lord Rischar. "There will be no way to trace it back to you. The interplanetary exchange will use the Bengari fleet. If we are to prove the exchange dangerous, we need to have information and a way to discredit those in charge."

Ubal went on for a few minutes about removing Lord

Travalla, but his persuasion was unnecessary. The faraway look in Lord Rischar's eyes bespoke much. He was already seeing himself sitting at the head of the Council of Unity. His words and attitude were much more courteous as he left.

"The sacred spirits guide you and protect you." He gave the traditional Shamaru farewell.

"May your path be prosperous and true," Ubal responded. Theirs was a parting of conspirators, not friends.

CHAPTER THIRTEEN
—EARTH—CANAVERAL SPACE CENTER

"Please fasten your seatbelts. We are approaching the Kennedy Space Center. You'll be able to see it on the right in a few minutes," said the pilot's voice as the sleek air cruiser made its descent over Florida. Kelli turned to look out the window of their transport, as did everyone except Ammie, who had toured the center half a dozen times. Their group filled less than half the seats in the private transport. The government was providing added security for the world-famous team of students headed for another planet. At first, all Kelli could see were clouds, but soon the plane dropped below them and the enormous complex of the Kennedy Space Center came into view, sprawling along a chunk of Florida's eastern coast.

"Wow, this place is enormous," Klaus Cole commented from the seat in front of her, echoing her thoughts. The large blond boy made no secret that his parents had insisted he join the team.

"NASA expanded the facility late in the 21st century when the UNWL took over control of all space exploration," Michael explained. "The United States gave up a sizable amount of prime resort land to accommodate the expansion."

Ammie asked, "The weather is so beautiful. Do you think

our schedule will allow us time to visit the beaches?"

"I don't think so, Ammie," Michael replied, "After the chaos of the last few weeks, I'm just happy to be here."

Kelli turned from the view outside her window to nod her agreement. News of the Aldebar Project had changed life at Barringer's Institute. It had threatened to become a virtual media circus, but the UNWL had kept the hordes of reporters and tele monitors at bay. The team had escaped Barringer's without being subjected to harassment by the media.

The next morning, Kelli studied the day's schedule. A session on the culture and peoples of Aldebar would be just after breakfast. That should be interesting. When she had begun her quest, she knew her father could be Aldebarian. Now she knew there were not one but seven sentient races on the planet. Who or what her father was had become much more complicated. She tried to imagine him as a silver skinned Degg, but it didn't seem to fit.

The sound of soft rapping caught her attention.

"Kelli, you up?" Duncan's voice called from the hallway.

"Yes, I'll be right out," she called, pleased that he had sought her company. She supposed that after years with Eric's company, it was normal that she would find interacting with adults easier. Duncan also knew her secrets. She slipped on her shoes and joined him.

Arriving in the dining hall, Kelli noticed Ammie holding court at the student's table. The girl seemed to enjoy being the center of attention, and her flair for dramatics made her a popular member of the team. Duncan steered Kelli to a table away from them, but she could still hear.

Ammie's excitement bubbled out as she spoke. "They're showing a transmission packet from Aldebar later. It will show the planet and the aliens there. My heart is beating so fast." She paused, breathing for effect. Then, in a lower, spookier tone, she continued, "What if the Aldebarians are horrible creatures?"

Duncan stood up with a concerned frown on his face as soon as he overheard Ammie's remark. He walked over to the table of laughing students and said, "Ammie, remember, on Aldebar we will be the aliens, and you may be the horrible creature."

His voice mimicked Ammie's exaggerated French accent, and the rebuke had an instant effect on the group. Kelli had never witnessed Duncan's temper before. Ammie apologized and then started eating in silence.

"Don't tell me I was too hard on Ammie," Duncan warned as he returned to their table.

"I didn't say a word, Dr. Meddars, not a word," Kelli replied, and took a slow sip of her coffee.

***

After breakfast, everyone met in conference room B-29, which turned out to be room B in Building 29. It was a short walk from the dining hall.

"Can any of you imagine a world with seven sentient species?" A young lieutenant built their anticipation before showing the first transmissions from Aldebar. "Believe it or not, you will soon live there."

When the first images began, an audible intake of air sounded throughout the room. A solitary figure appeared on the screen. The Aldebarian bowed and introduced himself as Rom Ectar, a diplomatic consort of the Second House of Aldebar. The amazement on Ammie's face left little doubt that the Degg exceeded everything her active imagination expected.

He appeared to be a humanoid biped with silvery skin, black almond-shaped eyes, and a mouth devoid of lips and teeth. When he welcomed them in perfect English, his mouth opening moved in ripples as he spoke.

"I give you greetings from Aldebar, from the House of Deggar, and from my people, the Degg. Our planet is one of beauty and diversity. Seven peoples inhabit Aldebar, and seven houses rule our peoples well. I received the honor to greet you because the open school you will attend is in Rishal, a trading city in my homeland of Deggar."

Rom Ectar's image faded away, and the screen filled with an aerial view of Rishal. To Kelli's inexperienced eye the city's buildings seemed to be marble, in varying tones of gray, silver, and white. They were diverse in shape, but few were Earth style rectangle boxes. The video panned the city for ten minutes, showing no other life forms. Rom Ectar appeared again and said, "I trust our translation has been successful. May your voyage here be fortuitous."

Kelli studied the stunned faces of the other students. For the first time, the reality of alien beings on another planet had pushed aside their dreams of adventure. The outcome of recruiting might have been different if this tape had been shown to students prior to recruitment. The alien even unsettled Kelli as she tried to imagine her father as one of the silver skinned Degg. Still, they had seen one of the alien races on Aldebar, and there were seven.

***

The second session of the morning proved less dramatic. A scientist explained that Aldebar was in the Taurus system orbiting the star Aldebaron. A much older lieutenant gave a brief and upbeat description. "Aldebaron is the brightest star in the Taurus System, and is 68.25 light years from Earth. We often refer to it as the Eye of Taurus. Aldebar is the largest planet orbiting Aldebaron, and as far as we know there are no other inhabited planets in their solar system. Using the Aldebarian technology to jump into hyperspace, the trip will last about three months. Rendezvousing on Alpha Three Station also cuts the original travel time by four months."

A murmur of excitement and anticipation once again shone on the faces of the students.

Kelli wanted to verify the accuracy of the information.

She could not monitor communications from Aldebar while at Cape Canaveral—she wanted to know why they had seen no other sentient species. But the risk of being detected was too great. Kelli touched the locket she was wearing. It contained the "Eric" program she would install on the alien network when they arrived.

***

The students' conversation at lunch centered on the video images of Aldebar, and Klaus teased Ammie by asking, "Are the Degg horrible enough for you, Ammie?" Her head nodded, and everyone laughed.

"What about those buildings?" Peter asked. "Didn't they appear to be solid marble?"

"Yes, they did," answered Niles Webster, adding, "Imagine carving an entire building out of one piece of marble."

"It looks like marble on screen, but it may be something different. We don't know its properties. They can fuse soft material to look like a solid piece of stone," Marla commented.

The students continued discussing theories as they walked to the next session.

***

The ninth exchange student, eighteen-year-old Liesel Edwards, skipped lunch to return to her room. She hummed as she sketched on a large canvas. Liesel began as the biggest surprise among the applicants for the Aldebar Project, and they had almost rejected her application. Professor Gentry had explained that all the other students were science majors or heading for diplomatic careers. "I'm gifted artistically," she had countered, "You must allow someone to study Aldebar's artistic culture." This argument won her a place on the team.

Liesel's tall, elegant figure and luxuriant red hair attracted attention from the young soldiers at the space center. Shy and quiet by nature, she paid little attention to their flirting. At Barringer's her dreamy, introverted nature had given her a reputation for being "not quite all there," but anyone familiar with her school records recognized her brilliant mind. She enjoyed spending most of her free time painting or writing in her journal. She stared at the canvas to make sure the lines were correct.

"You're going to be late for the afternoon session," Kelli chided.

"Sorry, I don't know why I can't keep up with the time," Liesel said, covering the canvas. She put away her art pencils and joined Kelli in the hall. With a smile, she accepted the bagel Ammie handed her. She had forgotten to eat, but they had remembered and brought her a snack.

"You get any thinner and the winds on Aldebar will blow you back home," Ammie teased.

"There are windstorms on Aldebar?" Liesel asked, munching on the bagel. She didn't remember reading about windstorms, but she found these training sessions boring and often daydreamed. She noticed a grin on Ammie's face and relaxed. Liesel would have preferred to finish painting, but she followed her roommate down the hall. Recalling the schedule, she skipped the optional tour of the Space Center scheduled for later in the afternoon.

The girls slipped into the meeting. Professor Gentry noted their late arrival by tapping his watch and frowning in their direction. Liesel squeezed Kelli's hand and whispered; "I'll explain that I made you late."

Liesel glanced in Professor Gentry's direction. There had been a tremendous fight when she applied for the exchange program. Her papa yelled and her mother cried. They were a close-knit family, one whose members didn't travel far from home, much less go clear across the galaxy. She had gotten her way, as she knew she would. Papa had given his permission over Mama's protest, and here she was following her dreams. She shifted in her seat, adjusted her skirt, and smoothed back her long red hair.

***

Professor Gentry glanced at his watch and frowned as the girls settled into their seats. He expected them to be on time, but Kelli was with Liesel Edwards. Liesel had a habit of losing track of time and being late to her classes. He would understand that she was trying to help Liesel stay on time.

One of NASA's scientists spoke. "We have confirmed the effectiveness of the immunizations the Aldebarians have provided, and we will monitor your health. The atmosphere on Aldebar can sustain human life. The oxygen content is thinner than on Earth, but it's richer in nitrogen and a few other trace elements. Other than experiencing a mild headache for the first couple of days, we don't expect you to have any problems adjusting. Are there questions?"

"Can you tell us what the climate is like?" Peter Wilkes asked. "It appeared to be dry with little vegetation."

"That's a good question," said the scientist. "It's hard to say for sure since our envoys haven't toured the entire planet, but our Aldebarian contacts tell us the temperature in Rishal is constant year-round."

Another scientist on the panel added, "A year on Aldebar comprises 452 thirty-hour days. The Rishal area has two short rainy seasons and three longer dry periods each year. I'm sure the climate varies planet wide, with tropical areas, deserts, temperate, and arctic zones. Does that answer your question?"

"Yes, thanks." Peter continued, "Any ideas how this affects the vegetation?"

"That's a question we hope you'll be able to answer when you return." The scientist smiled at the surprised faces of the students. "Remember, this is still a first contact situation."

Kelli studied Peter's face as he digested the statement. He was the most passionate about pioneering contact with an alien world. With his father's connections with the UNWL, Peter would be in a key position to become a liaison for a future diplomatic delegation to Aldebar, and a life of prestige.

"What about the other sentient beings on Aldebar?" Niles asked.

"Most of our contact has been with the Degg people," replied the scientist. "We have the complete approval of the Council of Unity, which is the Aldebarian equivalent of the UNWL. Again, we hope to find answers to these questions when you return."

Professor Gentry interrupted. "It seems like you're sending us into an almost unknown situation. What assurances do you have from the other sentient peoples of Aldebar? Will they welcome us? Have they guaranteed our safety? Will we be able to maintain any direct contact with Earth?"

"Calm down, Professor," replied the official. "We have the Aldebarian pledge of peace and cooperation. We will allow you liberal communications with Earth, considering the distance. Once a month we expect a detailed report on the program's progress. We will also be hosts to a group of Aldebarian students." Professor Gentry nodded but looked anything but pleased. The scientist said, "We'll meet after a brief break to take a tour of the Space Center."

Ammie seemed riveted by the interplay between the UNWL scientist and Professor Gentry. She whispered to Kelli, "Professor Gentry is very upset."

"Maybe he isn't feeling well," Liesel mumbled. "I'm going back to the room, Kelli. I'll join you at supper."

Kelli nodded and watched Liesel walking down the hall. She wondered how someone so bright could be unaware of what happened around her.

***

During the tour of the Space Center, they impressed Kelli with the quality of the technology. The space command personnel enjoyed showing off for a group of young people who understood the dynamics of space technology. One of the tour guides explained, "You're lucky. Fifty years ago, this would have been an uncomfortable voyage. Now we have gravity chambers in every shuttle, and travel is a breeze. You don't have to worry about heavy boots, suits, or weightlessness. It's much more like riding in an air cruiser now."

Peter asked, "Aren't things pretty cramped still?"

"You can see for yourself," the tour guide answered. "The shuttle has limited space, but I think you'll find the accommodations quite comfortable. Being cooped up for long periods of time can be stressful, so we've included activities to relieve boredom."

Their living area was a large open room with a kitchen and dining area. The recreational center was complete with exercise equipment and an automated walking track. Sleeping quarters comprised two rooms with the space age equivalent of bunk beds. They would crawl into these circular sleeping tubes. Once inside they were quite comfortable, and even had headphones and lights for reading and listening to music.

The tour was nearing its end, and Kelli thanked the guide for his excellent job. She had thought little about the voyage before. The thought of spending months in a spacecraft with eight other teenagers and two men would frighten the bravest woman. If she wasn't crazy now, she might well be by the time they reached Aldebar.

Duncan slipped an arm around her as they left the shuttle. "What's the matter? Did something he say frighten you?"

Kelli smiled and answered, "Just imagining being in there with everyone for months."

Duncan threw back his head and laughed. "You just thought about that? It's given me nightmares for weeks."

Kelli giggled and punched his arm. When something upset her, Duncan was always the first to notice. Kelli glanced at a clock. A nap before supper might help her get over several nights of short sleep.

She and Duncan walked together down the hallway leading to the rooms. As they passed Ammie and Marla's room, she heard male laughter mixed with Ammie's own. Kelli recognized Peter's voice. Trouble was beginning early. One of the first rules established with the students was that no guys went in the girl's bedrooms and vice versa, even in the daytime. She took a deep breath and knocked on the door.

Ammie jumped when the door slid open to reveal Kelli and Duncan. Peter stiffened and stood up.

Duncan leveled a stern gaze at Peter, but he refused to meet his eyes. "Peter, you're not supposed to be in this room."

Ammie broke in, pleading. "It's my fault, Professor. I invited Peter in, but we were looking at holographs."

Few people could resist Ammie's childlike charm, but unfortunately for her; Duncan Meddars was one of them. "You should have taken them to the recreation room. Don't let me find Peter in your room again.

Tears filled Ammie's large blue eyes. She sniffed, but soon realized the tears were being wasted and straightened her face. She answered, "Yes, sir."

Peter stood at attention; anxiety written on his face. Duncan would have to report the incident to Professor Gentry, who would no doubt decide on some suitable punishment. With a sigh of resignation, Peter promised, "It won't happen again."

"I'm sure it won't, Peter. Now, go to your room." Kelli stepped out of the door and a chastened Peter exited. Ammie followed, but Duncan shook his head. "You're to stay in your room until supper, and no sitting with Peter at meals for two days."

Kelli left as Ammie flopped down across the bed in frustration.

***

Kelli found a message from Dr. Granger waiting in her room. She wondered why he wanted her instead of Michael. The nap would have to wait while she returned the call. It took a few seconds to get a secure line outside the Space Center.

"Kelli, how are you? Is the training going well?' Dr. Granger asked.

"I'm great, just a little tired. Our training is going very well," Kelli answered. "What's up?"

"An old friend called. He says that someone's trying to locate you. You're to call him right away for details."

"That can't be right. No one would be looking." Kelli's stomach lurched with fear.

"It sounds serious. Can you get to a secure line?"

"I think so. I'll get back to you after I find out what's going on. Please, don't worry," Kelli said to reassure Dr. Granger.

It took almost an hour to secure a line to Eric. His haggard face appeared on the screen. He looked as if he hadn't had a good night's sleep.

"Someone's tracking you, and they've traced you to Barringer's," he said.

Eric's panic forced Kelli to remain calm. "Who is it? I'm working with the UNWL."

"You're not working with the UNWL. We are both high on the most wanted list. I can find one clear lead, a phone number at UNWL Security Headquarters. I checked it out and came up negative. The communications port is in an empty basement office. It shouldn't still be active."

"So, it's not the UNWL?" Kelli asked, twisting her gold chain until it cut against her neck.

"It's not the UNWL. It may be someone there working on their own. Get out while you can," Eric shouted.

"I can't abandon the project now. Find out more."

The conversation ended with an argument. Eric yelled about people who didn't take advice. Tears clouded Kelli's eyes as she left her room, and she collided with Duncan in the hall.

"Whoa. What's wrong?" Duncan steadied her and kept an

arm around her shoulder as they walked.

"Someone is after me. They may be here any minute. Two weeks before we leave and it's over."

"Calm down. Who's after you?"

"I don't know, but they've traced me to Barringer's."

Duncan stopped walking. He faced Kelli and tilted her head up. His expression became more serious and calmer. His eyes pierced into hers. "Don't worry. You'll come out of this smelling like a rose."

Kelli pulled back with a start. "You're psychic. Why haven't you told me before?"

"I promised Michael that I wouldn't use the ability on this trip," Duncan answered. "I didn't realize how hard it would be to control my powers; it's like putting on a blindfold and being told not to peek for three years."

By the time they reached the dining room, Kelli felt better. She would warn Michael, but she wouldn't run away. They would have to force her off the shuttle.

***

A week later, everyone gathered in the dining area ready to eat, except Liesel. She was late again. The wait staff served salad on chilled silver plates. The students ordered soft drinks and fruit juice. Liesel, spattered with paint and breathless, rushed in carrying a large, covered canvas.

"I'm sorry I'm late. I had to finish my first painting."

She whipped back the cover and there stood a remarkable likeness of Rom Ectar. Cradled in his arms, he held the skyline of Rishal. In the background, the planet Aldebar filled the canvas. It was a magnificent painting, and remarkable because Liesel had created it from a memory of a single transmission.

The dining room exploded in applause. Students, professors, and Space Center personnel alike voiced their appreciation. She smiled and gave a small curtsy before placing the painting on an empty table and joining Kelli.

After the meal, a young lieutenant approached Liesel. "Admiral Berney wants to speak to you, Miss Edwards. If you are available, I can show you the way."

"Me? I don't think I know an Admiral Berney, but I'll be glad to go talk to him. I'll tell Professor Gentry where I'll be."

The lieutenant waited and escorted her down the twisting hall to the admiral's office. Once there, he bowed and returned to his station. Admiral Berney joined Liesel in his office.

"Hello young lady. I've had no less than five calls in the last thirty minutes praising this painting of yours. Is there any chance I can see it?"

"You want to see my painting?" asked Liesel. She was talented, but never dreamed her work would cause such a stir.

"Yes, I do." The admiral laughed. "Would you be willing to let us display it here at the center while you're gone?"

"It would honor me," Liesel replied, her heart pounding with joy and excitement. They shook hands and agreed to have the Space Center purchase a suitable frame. Liesel ran back to her room to tell Rebecca the news.

***

By the next evening, the painting hung in the main foyer of the headquarters building. Liesel, Ammie, and Kelli were admiring it when a uniformed officer approached them.

"Are you Kelli Royal?" he said.

She fought the urge to run, steeled herself, and answered, "Yes, can I help you?"

"These are for you." He handed Kelli a long narrow box, bowed, and left.

Kelli ripped open the box. Inside were a dozen perfect yellow roses. Lifting them out, she breathed the delicate sweet scent. Ammie and Liesel squealed with excitement.

"Oh, they are so beautiful. Who are they from?" Ammie asked, peering at the unopened card on the box.

"Give her a chance to find out," Liesel interrupted, and

took Ammie's arm. "Let's let Kelli enjoy her flowers in peace. She will tell us who they're from later. Won't you, Kelli?"

"That depends on who sent them," Kelli laughed. "A few secrets might enhance my reputation."

The girls walked down the hall. If anyone had the scoop on Kelli's love life, it would be Ammie, and she knew nothing. Kelli knew that because there was nothing to know.

She waited until they were out of sight and then walked all the way back to her room before opening the note. The note read:

Kelli,
May Aldebar be the lucky star shining in the heavens above you.
Best wishes,
General Gregory Edwards
UNWL Headquarters

CHAPTER FOURTEEN
—ALDEBAR—SHAMARU HOMELAND

Shual clutched his meditation stone and sought tranquility as the transport rose into the mountains of Shamar. One was, of course, not afraid—Degg did not fear. He was unfamiliar with Shamaru transports and had a natural preference for the desert lowlands of Deggar. He shook his head and watched as they rose higher. The Shamaru had carved their cities into the mountain peaks of their homeland. Long ago, they could only be reached by the Shamaru with their great wings. If his memory was correct, these had served as defensible fortresses during the Great Wars. Of course, his memory was seldom incorrect. He relaxed.

Lord Ravon had summoned him to the highest of the mountain cities for a meeting. Ravon didn't trust even the most secure communications these days, and who could blame him? Weeks and weeks of investigating had uncovered the source of the political attacks. Another alarming fact had also surfaced. An anonymous message had warned of an attempt to destroy the transport carrying the student delegation to Earth.

Once inside, Lord Ravon and two ranking members of the High Council greeted Shual and listened to his report.

"We can change our transport vessel at the last minute," the high lord of Deggar offered. "I will arrange with the Bengari

Fleet."

Lord Ravon perused the report. "The threat seems to be against me, not against the students or the Earth people."

"One's wisest course would be to warn the Earth delegation of the threat," the high lord of Deggar said.

"The Earth government would back out of the exchange, which may be what these radicals want," Lord Travalla broke in. "Is there any way to protect the students without causing undue alarm?"

Shual spoke, avoiding the eyes of his old friend, Lord Ravon. "Noble lords, this most humble worker deleted certain information from the files as a precaution. Our records now show that we have moved the departure back to its original date and location. This one also suggests Lord Ravon announce that he will not be a member of the delegation."

"Good thinking. Anyone planning the attack will wait until it is out of Aldebar's atmosphere. When they realize Lord Ravon isn't on board, they won't even try." Lord Travalla's eyes shined with purple fire. His silver hair attested to his many years of service as head of the High Council.

One could see Lord Ravon struggling to keep his temper in check. Shual grew faint when Ravon said, "I don't enjoy giving in to terrorists, but I won't put everyone else in danger. Would you consider letting Senior Programmer Shual take my place? He would need a cover story. Perhaps Lord Hun of your house will arrange something."

"You speak wisely, Lord Ravon. I will make the changes," the high lord answered.

"But this one is not desirous of going off world," Shual said, and shook his head. He had little hope that his words would carry any weight with the high lord.

"You're the best communication expert we have, and one of the few people I can trust," said Lord Ravon.

"That does not offer this one great comfort," Shual said.

"Nonsense, Shual, you are a resourceful individual, and most honorable," Lord Ravon added.

Such praise from the Shamaru lord touched Shual, and he lowered his voice and answered. "All Degg are honorable, my lord Ravon."

CHAPTER FIFTEEN
—Space—Aboard Voyager Nine

Voyager-9 launched without delay on a bright spring morning. The crew and twelve passengers spent the first hour harnessed on acceleration couches. Once the transport was free of the Earth's atmosphere, they got up and moved about in the main compartment.

The students crowded around the viewer, watching Earth grow smaller behind them. Not even the best videos could match the sheer beauty of the experience. The faces of the students shone with excitement and wonder. They mirrored what Kelli was feeling inside. The plump figure of Klaus Cole turned away, blinking back tears. She reached out a hand to touch him.

"It's too late to go back now," Klaus said. Homesickness was hitting him early and hard. Kelli reached up to touch his curly blond hair and his pale round cheeks. Klaus was the baby of the group. He wasn't the youngest, but he was immature. The baby of his family, Klaus had led a very sheltered life before coming to Barringer's and later to the team. He had confided in Kelli that his parents were behind his application.

"Would you want to give up this opportunity?" she asked.

"No, I guess not," Klaus answered. He turned back to the viewscreen, wiping away a stray tear. "My mom makes the best strudel cake."

"I'll bet she does." Kelli laughed and hugged his broad shoulders. Klaus would have to adjust to alien cuisine soon. And if he lost a few pounds in the change, that would be a bonus to his health.

It surprised the other students that Kelli tinted her irises, but Ammie declared them magnificent. Now, with her hair hanging loose and shining around her shoulders, she knew she looked different. *If only they knew how different*, she thought.

"Kelli, can I ask you a question?" Ammie walked over to the automated track where Kelli was doing the recommended five-mile workout. The cool down segment began, and the track slowed to a walking pace.

"Sure, Ammie. We can talk while I do the last laps," Kelli answered. She wanted to build a trusting relationship with the girls. Ammie was sophisticated, and yet had such an aura of innocence and vulnerability.

"Where did you go to school?" Ammie began. "You came to Barringer's to join the student exchange, but where did you come from? You are more advanced than any of the students and several professors at Barringer's. Even Professor Gentry listens to you like an adult."

Kelli hesitated. How could she answer Ammie without lying? She opted for an edited version of the truth. "For the last four years, I didn't go anywhere. I had a private teacher. When I read about the Aldebar Project, I contacted Dr. Granger about joining."

"That's amazing," Ammi said.

"No, I still had to take the tests and make the team," Kelli answered.

"Is that why you always act so serious, like an old woman sometimes?"

"If I promise not to act like your mom, will you promise not to act eighteen?"

"But I want Peter to like me."

"Peter is a smart guy. Give him the chance to see the real you."

***

The month-long trip to Alpha Three began. That lifted a great weight from Kelli. For the first time in months, she didn't fear a UNWL agent would appear to whisk her away. Duncan smiled and called her beautiful when they met in the hall. With little to do on the shuttle, she found it harder to keep her feelings in perspective.

"Good morning, Duncan," Kelli said. They were both early risers, and often shared coffee before the other team members crawled out of their bunks. Kelli masked the bitter taste of the instant coffee with creamer and sugar.

"I never thought I'd miss Karl's coffee," Duncan joked as he tried to make his more palatable. The meteor shower they were passing made a spectacular display on the viewscreen. They watched it in silence for a while, content with enjoying each other's presence.

"It doesn't seem real, does it?" Duncan was the first to break the silence. "We're here thousands of miles in space, and it seems like a movie."

"It's the waiting. Once we rendezvous at Alpha Three, we'll be busy again."

Perhaps it was the lights from the meteors flickering in his eyes, or the special way he had of looking at her that weakened her control. When he reached out, she didn't pull back. The kiss was gentle.

"Do you think we should do this?" Kelli gazed at him.

"I think we should not be doing this," Duncan answered, keeping his arms around her. "And we won't do it again."

"Why? I don't think Aldebar has a law against kissing."

"It has nothing to do with the law, it's you and me. Being involved wouldn't be a good idea. This is a long voyage, and we'll be on Aldebar for three years."

"I thought we were talking about a kiss, not a serious relationship," Kelli said.

"Can you see us having a casual fling?" Duncan answered.

"No, I guess I hadn't thought about it. Three years is a long time."

"I know; don't think I haven't thought about that."

"I can't promise I'll even be returning to Earth," Kelli continued, looking in his eyes.

Duncan blinked in surprise. His eyes darkened to forest green. "What do you mean?"

"My feelings could change. About Earth. About my past. I try not to think about it. Who knows who or what my father is or was? I have three years to find out."

"What if you find nothing?"

Kelli pulled away from him. "I know the answer is there."

"You could have a job at Barringer's, and a home with people who care about you."

"Thanks. I don't know if I'm cut out for teaching."

Kelli moved back to the viewer and, instead of joining her, Duncan went over to the auto track. He was having a vigorous workout when the others joined them.

***

Another week of the voyage passed. The limited space and quiet routine bored the students. They grew restless. Michael, Duncan, and the ship's crew held impromptu classes on astronomy and space travel. The crew even allowed Niles and Peter to help with their duties.

Niles spent most of his time with the navigations officer and pilot. His quick reflexes and sharp mind made him a natural whiz at the control panel. He was observing the navigations officer when the primary computer system malfunctioned. The pilot flashed an alert and the entire five-man crew converged in the small bridge area. Niles stood watching near the bridge; out of the way, but close enough to see and hear. He watched the crew's concern turn to panic over the next hour as they tried and failed to correct the computer problem. Niles could tell that they were drawing on all their training and failing.

The pilot walked past, and Niles asked, "Can you fix it?"

"I'll be honest. It's not good. The commander is going to send an emergency transmission to Earth. If we don't get the navigational computer online soon, they'll have to send another transport to rescue us."

Niles let out a low whistle. "Rescue? We're in danger? What happened?"

"Hell if I know. The entire system's coming apart. Life support's online, but we don't know for how long. The commander thinks it may be sabotage."

"Sabotage? How? I can't see how anyone could get past security at Canaveral."

"A mega-virus infected the system and someone activated it later. It'll take one of the computer geniuses at command central to debug."

"You need a computer genius?"

"Yeah, but they won't haul this shuttle back. We're too far out, and they have newer shuttles in the system. It would cost too much."

Niles debated his next words. He didn't want to get into trouble with Professor Gentry. "Look, I don't know if this will help, but we have someone on our team that might debug your computer."

"Someone on your team is familiar with advanced systems?"

"I think so. I overheard Professor Gentry once say that Kelli had designed cognitive programs."

The pilot gave Niles an incredulous look. "At this point we're willing to try anything."

Niles hurried Kelli to the control area, explaining as much

as possible along the way. The commander greeted them.

***

"Niles tells us you've worked on advanced computer systems."

"I've done some design work." Kelli shot Niles a glowering look. How had he known about her work?

"We're getting desperate, and Niles says you've designed cognitive-chips. If you can do that, you're better than good," the commander replied.

It took a few minutes for Kelli to digest what the commander was saying, and part of her still couldn't believe that Niles knew about her work with cognizant chips. Did he know about Eric? She looked at the commander's anxious face. "I'm not sure I can help. I'd have to work alone."

The commander's face registered his feelings about that stipulation. But she was firm. She didn't want anyone to know she had an L-Seven chip on board. The possibility of the mission being canceled and having to return to Earth convinced him to agree.

"You'll have about three hours before I have to contact Canaveral."

"It's that bad?"

"It's worse. If we drift into that group of asteroids, we're dead."

"I'll get to work."

Kelli seated herself at the command terminal while the commander explained to the crew that they needed to leave the area for a while. She could see the reluctance on their faces, but they were also used to following orders.

Kelli began by entering a few simple commands. The screen filled with gibberish. It looked like a simple virus. One of the crew should have been able to isolate and destroy the program. She tried a few routine procedures for isolating the virus. The screen went blank and Kelli had to reboot to get it to come back on. The gibberish returned, despite the reboot. Kelli placed her L-Seven on the control panel. That should guarantee Eric access. She entered her password. She expected to see its menu fill the screen. Eric was immune to any kind of virus. The screen remained blank. For some unknown reason, the system was rejecting the L-Seven chip.

"The commander wants to know how it's going." Niles' voice gave her a start. She had not noticed that he had walked up behind her. Kelli tried to cover up the tiny hologram hovering above the panel. "Is that an intel hologram?"

"Yes, but you never saw this. No one hears about this. Do you understand, Niles?" Kelli showed the L-7 chip she had placed on the computer.

"Sure, you can trust me. I've got lips of steel."

"Good. I helped design this myself, and the UNWL frowns on that sort of thing."

Niles rolled his eyes and nodded. "Unauthorized artificial intelligence programs above L2 are illegal."

"Very illegal, Niles, so forget you saw this one." Kelli stressed her point and then changed the subject. "The shuttle's control system won't accept the chip. Something in the virus must block it. I need uninfected access."

"The life support systems are working. I heard the pilot say we'd all be dead in a matter of minutes if the virus shut them down."

"I can't disable life support for the same reason."

"What about waste disposal? That's in the life support system. We could function without that for a little while."

"Niles, you're a genius. Ask the commander for the schematics of the control panel, and hurry."

Niles returned in minutes. He was out of breath, but he had the blueprints. He held them up while Kelli's finger keyed in commands. She had to be careful not to damage any essential programs. She moved back to the command terminal. Holding her breath, she tried to access the life support system. The system was online. A listing of functions appeared on the screen. Kelli was unaware of Niles' victory dance behind her. She breathed a sigh of relief and wiped sweat from her forehead. She selected the waste disposal function. The cognizant-chip's holographic image appeared and a simulated voice, patterned after Eric Fendler's, greeted her.

"Hello, Eric. You're in the life support systems of a space shuttle, series 49523. A virus has infected the shuttle's computer system. Can you identify the virus?"

"Processing.... The virus does not conform to known parameters. I will analyze the virus now and provide a profile."

"Eric, you may proceed." Kelli stretched. Niles stood behind her. He was speechless. She smiled and squeezed his hand.

"Processing.... Warning! The virus is cognizant. The shuttle is in danger."

"Eric, there is no such thing as a cognizant-virus."

"The virus is cognizant. It fits all requirements for classification as a cognizant design. My analysis is correct."

"I believe you, Eric. Can you isolate and contain the virus?"

"Processing.... The virus has assimilated the standard programs. Containment is not possible."

"How can we get rid of the virus?"

"Processing.... Eric Fendler added a search and destroy function to my program. It erases cognizant programs so the UNWL could find no evidence of your research. It may work against the virus."

"Won't that erase the shuttle's programs with the virus?" Kelli's throat was dry. She moistened her lips with her tongue.

"Yes, but if I am successful, I can reprogram the shuttle's computer to 99.8% accuracy," the holographic voice of Eric Fendler replied.

"What happens if you're not successful?" Niles spoke up

for the first time.

"Accessing voice identification.... Hello, Niles Webster. Your question is being processed.... If I cannot erase the virus, it will infect my program. I will cease to exist. This shuttle's drift will take it into an asteroid group. There is a high probability of our destruction. The estimated time of life support failure is —"

"We don't require that information, Eric," Kelli interrupted. She could tell that Niles was getting frightened; it scared her too. "What are the chances of destroying the virus?"

"That is unknown. Assuming that my design is superior to that of the virus, the odds are in our favor. However, that assumption could be wrong. I base that on the logic that one would not build a short-term virus with the power and complexity of a cognizant program."

"That makes sense to me. Go ahead with search and destroy."

"Implementing...." The screen went blank.

Kelli didn't panic. Eric had entered the infected systems. All they could do now was wait and pray that the L-Seven chip could do the job. Kelli realized she was very thirsty. "Niles, will you get me a mint soda from the beverage compartment?"

"Sure, Miss Royal." Niles backed out of the control area, his eyes glued to the terminal screen. He stumbled over the step up to the main shuttle area, just managing not to fall. Niles ran to the beverage compartment and grabbed two drinks and hurried back toward the control room.

"Niles, what's going on? The commander says you're repairing the shuttle's computer." Duncan Meddars stepped between Niles and the command area. "I'll take these. I need to talk to Kelli."

"But Kelli asked...," Niles protested. He looked up at the scowl on Duncan Meddars' face. "Yes, sir. She wants the mint soda."

Kelli heard the exchange behind and greeted Duncan with

a nod. "I hate this waiting. Something must be wrong with Eric."

"Who's Eric?"

The anger in Duncan's voice startled Kelli. She turned the swivel chair around to face him. Their eyes locked. Duncan handed her the mint drink, and Kelli took a long swallow of the cold beverage. She steered the conversation in another direction. She filled him in on what she was doing, at least part of it. "I'm helping the commander with a computer problem. There's a virus in the control system. The waste disposal system will be offline for a few minutes."

"Who's Eric?" Duncan repeated his question. Neither noticed the terminal screen come on again. Duncan took hold of Kelli's arm. "I thought you were through keeping secrets."

"Please take your hands off Kelli."

"Eric, you're back." Kelli felt exuberant. Duncan and Michael could rant all they wanted. Bringing the cognizant on board had saved their lives, and the lives of every student on the shuttle. "You worried me."

"No need for concern. I destroyed the cognizant virus. To reprogram the shuttle's navigational functions, I must access the guidance chip E-237 position. If you enter the code, you will find the correct position in the upper left corner. Dr. Meddars, you might be more comfortable if you sit down."

"How does it know I'm standing?" Duncan asked. He walked over and almost touched the holographic projection.

"That is a good question, Dr. Meddars. NASA equipped Voyager-9 with many recorders, whose function is to relay pictures back to Earth. By accessing them, I can monitor eighty-five percent of the shuttle's interior."

Duncan nodded. He rubbed his hand across the screen. The hologram disappeared. "Where did he go?"

"I'm putting Eric in the command console," Kelli answered.

Duncan looked at the tiny silver dot resting on her fingertip. That dot had been talking to him. That dot was reprogramming a navigational system.

"Reprogramming complete. The shuttle is now functioning above specifications. Is there anything else you require?" Eric's flickering colors returned to the screen. Duncan once again ran his hand across the screen, as if to touch Eric.

"Are you alive?" He addressed the question to Eric this time.

"Define the parameters of life, Dr. Meddars. I am cognizant. However, I am not a living being."

Kelli had been listening to the conversation. Duncan seemed to appreciate the program on a different level. She wished she could give them more time to get acquainted. "Eric, come out now. Thanks for your help."

She returned the chip to the safety of the hidden compartment in her locket. The shuttle headed back on its correct course, ready to rendezvous at Alpha Three.

CHAPTER SIXTEEN
—SPACE STATION ALPHA THREE

The Bengarian ship hovered above the space station like an enormous bat with wings extended in flight. It measured six times the size of Voyager 9. The earth students crowded around the view screen, eager to see the alien vessel that would carry them to Aldebar. Kelli glanced at Duncan, who was staring at the vessel, transfixed by its size and elegance. He turned and their eyes met. The look of excitement and wonder on his face spoke louder than the cheers of the students beside him.

"She's huge. Look at the wingspan," he said, and reached a hand toward the screen. "Can you imagine the power needed to lift that thing off the ground?"

"They must have air docks outside the main gravitational pull of their planet," said Niles.

"Maybe it's constructed from a super lightweight metal," Peter added.

Soon everyone chimed in, and it filled the shuttle with the sound of excited chatter. Liesel sketched with charcoal and pastel chalk, trying to capture the scene on canvas. Because of the shuttle's sensitive ventilation system, she had packed away her pastels and oil paints during the voyage.

"That looks marvelous," Rebecca commented, looking

over her shoulder.

"It's the best I can do with these. I'm sick to death of charcoal," Liesel replied.

"Get your things together, girls. We'll be docking in thirty minutes," said Professor Gentry.

Kelli walked over to Liesel and offered to help gather her art supplies. Rebecca nodded and walked toward the sleeping quarters. Kelli had noticed a chill in Rebecca's attitude towards her. She didn't remember saying or doing anything that might have offended the good-natured girl.

On Alpha Three, two Degg representatives waited to greet them. They looked much frailer than Kelli had imagined after seeing the holotapes. Both stood six feet tall, but were thinner than Ammie's slight frame.

"Welcome Dr. Gentry, Dr. Meddars, students. This one is Rom Ishma, a representative of the Degg Homeland." He nodded toward the other Degg. "This is my assistant, Shual. Your arrival brings us much joy. One hopes your voyage was a pleasant one." Rom Ishma bowed, and Shual brought out a large gleaming decanter that held a dark blue drink. Nodding his head, Rom Ishma poured some dark liquid into a glass. He handed it to Michael, who hesitated before taking a sip.

"It's good. Not like anything I've ever tasted." He laughed as they handed Duncan a glass.

Duncan took a long drink and with a sputtered cough said, "That's got a bite. You should sip it."

As he handed the drink to Kelli, a firm but gentle silver hand grabbed his wrist. Shual removed the glass from his hand and returned it to Rom Ishma.

"Rube is a man's drink," he explained, and bowed toward Kelli. "I intend no disrespect, Miss Royal. They make Rube with the milk of the male Gelt cattle. It contains a hormone like testosterone. You would not find its effects as pleasant as your friends do. It is a gift from the captain of the Bengarian vessel we travel on."

"I take no offense, friend." Kelli extended her hands to the Degg leader. "You say the vessel is Bengarian. What does that mean?

"Pardon, one forgets how little information they gave you about Aldebar. Bengar is the Fifth House of Aldebar. The ordinal number denotes when they joined the Council of Unity, not their importance or status. They are renowned for their technology, strength, and valor. Alas, we do not know them for their diplomacy. A simple wine everyone could enjoy would have been more appropriate."

"I expect to learn many of Aldebar's customs." Kelli smiled, accepting the implied apology. Peter was looking at Professor Gentry and then at the decanter. With a firm shake of his head, Michael told him that a drink was out of the question. Kelli turned back to their Degg hosts. She reached out and took Shual's silvery arm and started making small talk. The Degg's skin felt like the warm and dry touch of a snake after it has laid in the sun.

***

Duncan Meddars tried to shake the effects of the Rube. He felt his heart racing and the blood rushing through his veins. His muscles ached to move faster, to release the pent-up energy. Kelli's scent wafted across the room. He tried not to think about her. Signaling to Michael, he moved a discrete distance before speaking.

"Are you experiencing any unusual effects from that drink?"

"Damn right. I'll have a word with the captain about this," said Michael.

"Perhaps in their culture an aphrodisiac is an appropriate gift."

Michael said, "I hope not. I don't think I could handle any more gifts."

"But it has export potential, if the Aldebarians care to set up trade negotiations," Duncan said, to lighten the mood.

Michael face's reddened as he failed to control a smile. "Oh, yes. I think they will find Earth a very lucrative market for Rube."

***

Kelli's mellow mood turned tense. The Aldebarians had set up a bio scan chamber on Alpha Three. There had been no mention of this in any communications with the UNWL. Michael Gentry joined her as Rom Ishma explained.

"A small safety measure, this test identifies viruses and bacteria in the breath particles. We seek to protect our people and yours from an epidemic."

"Did we subject your students to such a procedure?" Michael's tone was a sign that he knew the answer.

"I was not aware of Earth having such a medical device," Rom Ishma countered. "Our students went through a complete decontamination procedure."

"We must take your word on that."

"The Degg do not lie. It is not part of our nature." Rom Ishma stiffened. He nodded toward Duncan. "He knows. Ask him if you do not believe me."

"What does Dr. Meddars have to do with this?" Michael asked.

"He sees," Rom Ishma said. "Dr. Meddars is your seer. He can tell if I am lying."

Kelli's eyes widened in surprise. She looked at Duncan. They could not deny his psychic ability. Michael looked from Rom Ishma to Duncan.

"He's telling the truth, Mike, though how he knows I can read him is beyond me. I haven't used my ability once on this voyage," said Duncan.

"Your seer doesn't use his ability, how odd," Shual commented. He was standing next to Kelli, observing the exchange.

Kelli placed a hand on Michael's arm to get his attention. "If Rom Ishma says the tests are safe, his word is good." Kelli nodded toward Shual.

Michael said, "We mean no offense. Our government has placed these students in our care. It would bring us dishonor if we failed to protect them."

"Of course. We are much alike then." Rom Ishma bowed. "Failure to serve you would bring us dishonor."

Tensions eased and everyone, except Rom Ishma, helped to load luggage onto the transport that would carry them to the Bengari vessel. The bio scans revealed that the team members carried no dangerous bacteria or virus forms. They declared everyone safe to board.

***

Kelli sat clasping her hands as the shuttle made the brief trip to the Aldebarian vessel. Everyone seemed in silent anticipation of entering the unknown. There could be no turning back now.

"Come," said Shual when the doors on the transport opened. Rom Ishma led the way, his head high and his pace slow and ceremonial. A Bengari honor guard, three on each side, stood at attention as they walked down the steps and into the boarding area.

Kelli admired the large, well-muscled guards. At first glance, they could have passed for men. Long copper colored hair hung down their backs. V-shaped brows arched above brilliant yellow eyes. Their faces tapered out with large, high-bridged noses. Their skin appeared smooth, bronze, and hairless. When Rom Ishma spoke, Kelli could understand him, but not their reply. Shual was quick to explain.

"Rom Ishma and I both wear translators. You will find yours in Dr. Gentry's cabin. Our world is diverse. Each homeland has its own language and hundreds of dialects. Long ago we found it expedient to develop a single common language for use when dealing with other peoples and cultures. That language is Barric. The device will translate everything you say into Barric. You will hear our words in English. When someone speaks one of the other languages, the translator will change it to Barric, then to English. This will cause a slight sound delay, but is the best we can offer for now."

Kelli was so busy looking around that she missed some of Shual's words. She decided that admitting this might be disrespectful, so she smiled, nodding agreement with whatever he had said. If he was aware of her ruse, he kept the knowledge to himself. Kelli noted what appeared to be ventilation ducts. A white mist floated from them, dissipating into the room. There were visual monitors in the upper corners of the room, and communication panels by each door.

"The ship's captain has asked that you dine with him. They will serve the high meal in two hours. Will that give you sufficient time to unpack?" asked Shual, and nodded to Kelli, Michael, and Duncan.

"Yes, and I'm eager to meet the captain," Michael replied. "I'm sure we will all be ready for a break and for food by then."

They followed Shual to their quarters while Rom Ishma continued talking to Michael in a soft tone. She could no longer follow the conversation. When she turned her head. Shual seemed to study her.

He stopped in front of a silver door. "This is your room, Ms. Royal. Someone will come for you when it is time for the high meal."

Giving in to an impulse, she imitated his formal bow. "Please call me Kelli."

The silver tint of his skin darkened, and his eyes lowered. "This one is most honored that you hold him in such high regard."

Kelli blushed, realizing that she had been too forward.

After a few moments of awkward silence, Shual nodded

toward the open door and said, "I will leave you to unpack, Kelli. Someone will come when it is time for the high meal." The door slid closed and Kelli opened her luggage. She jumped when the door panel buzzed. Relieved, she heard Michael's voice on the other side.

"Open." She voiced the simple command. Michael entered and handed her a translator. He looked at her with a frown. She was almost afraid to ask what was wrong because she already knew.

"Duncan told you about the cognizant, right?" Kelli began. He raised an eyebrow in response. "I know it's not legal, but it has a built-in safety function. The minute the UNWL tries to examine it, poof, it erases itself. Don't look at me like that. How did you think I was going to do my research?"

"I knew about the cognizant chip," Michael answered.

"You knew I had a cognizant chip? How?" Kelli's voice rose an octave. She didn't quite believe him.

"One day a friend of yours visited Barringer's. You were not on campus, so he left some forged authorization papers with Dr. Granger. He assumed that since you were working with us, you trusted us enough to be honest about what you were planning. Silly man to make that kind of mistake."

Michael's sarcasm hit Kelli hard. She trusted Michael, Dr. Granger, or Duncan. She was used to working alone, had always found it safer not to include others in her plans. But her friends depended on her honesty. Kelli knew she had let them down, again.

After Kelli berated herself for a few minutes, Michael was ready to let the matter go. Now that it was out in the open, he wanted to know more about the program.

"What level cognizant design are we talking about?" Michael asked. He considered himself familiar with the field. He had never worked on the design of these super chips, but he had operated a cognizant program twice in his career. Both times had been while helping the UNWL on a research project.

Kelli breathed a sigh of relief. Michael unclenched his hands and relaxed his shoulders. Her work with cognizant chips was one of her passions, one she loved to talk about. She said, "Eric, that's what I call him, is a level seven cognizant chip."

"Level seven? I wasn't aware that research had gone beyond level four."

"We went beyond that years ago. But you're talking about government research and development, aren't you? They're so far behind that I've stopped keeping up with most of their work."

"Behind whom? No, never mind. I don't want to know." Michael shook his head.

"Would you like to see Eric?" Kelli offered. "I have limited the function of the cognizant chip in my portable computer, but accessing the Bengari ship's computer is out of the question. This is the best I can do until we reach Rishal."

"Sure, we have a few minutes."

Kelli inserted the cognizant chip into the computer's processor without activating the hologram function. The flickering color patterns appeared on the screen.

"So, what does it do?"

"Voice identification activated.... Dr. Michael Gentry. Is there something I can do for you, Dr. Gentry?"

"Can you keep Miss Royal out of trouble?" Michael winked at Kelli.

Kelli laughed. "You can disregard that question, Eric."

"They programmed me as a protection device. Does that include keeping her out of trouble?"

"I never programmed that function." The ramifications of such a function alarmed Kelli. Eric Fendler must have changed the program without her knowledge. "Eric, define parameters of protection. Define danger."

"What's wrong? I thought you would be pleased to have some extra protection." Michael Gentry frowned at her flying fingers and panicked reaction.

"The Eric program may sound human, but it's still a program," Kelli tried to explain. "It thinks, but it doesn't have emotions or morals. It carries out programming."

"Meaning in this situation?"

"It would eliminate any perceived danger, using the most effective means at its disposal. Here in my portable computer, it has no way to carry out this function. If it could access the ship's computer, it might switch off life support to an area, interrupt navigational control, whatever it felt necessary to protect me."

"Can you reprogram it?" Michael studied the screen is if the image were the program. The word "destroy" hung unspoken in the air.

"If I can't, I'll erase the core memory net and build a whole new program."

The door panel buzzed. Duncan Meddars' smile vanished when he saw Michael Gentry at the computer screen. "Ho, Eric. It's good to see you, friend."

"Voice identification activated.... Dr. Meddars, it is good to hear your voice. I cannot view you, but I have a photographic imprint of your likeness on file. Where are we?"

"We're on the Bengari vessel headed for Aldebar."

"You should link me with the ship's computer. This location is not suitable for cognizant functioning."

"Sorry pal, this is your home for a while," Michael answered.

"It is small, Dr. Gentry. I will be of little use from this location."

"I'm going to perform maintenance on your program, and then I'll move you back to home base." Kelli always referred to her elaborate computer system as home base. This seemed to satisfy Eric's logic. The three humans headed for some dinner. On the way, Kelli filled Duncan in on the problem with Eric's program.

***

On another level of the Bengari vessel, a briefing began. The Bengari captain, Rom Ishma, and a high ranking Shamaru official were present.

"The shuttle arrived at Alfa Three in time to rendezvous with our ship. Any word on who planted the virus?" asked the Shamaru.

"Nothing definite, my lord," Ishma's voice hesitated. Dealing with the Shamaru ambassador always made him nervous.

"Is there any reason to suspect that it was anything other than one of their political factions trying to cause trouble?" the ambassador said, as if voicing his own suspicions.

"Do you mean that one of our enemies could have sabotaged the Earth shuttle?" the Bengari captain, Raggion, interjected.

"Are you saying that Lord Tobul suspects one of our operatives of being a traitor?" Ishma asked.

"Of course, he does." Raggion laughed. "A Shamaru suspects everyone. It's in their blood."

"Enough." An older Bengari dressed in diplomatic robes stood up. "Lord Travalla is a member of the High Council. He has enemies. The decision to contact Earth was not unanimous."

"I cannot say who tried to disable the shuttle. When we ran a scan of the computer, they had destroyed all traces of the virus. However, we found evidence of a high-level program in the memory banks. From the residual pattern, it is beyond current Earth technology. It was used to destroy the virus, and now it's gone." Rom Nebbar looked from the Bengari captain to the two lords.

"What happened to it?" The Bengari, Lord Halvati, spoke again, his voice old, but still filled with power and authority.

"The Earth records say nothing about this program. The students seem to think someone named Kelli Royal destroyed the virus," Ishma explained.

"The female? What would a student be doing with such advanced technology?" Lord Tobul's eyes blazed like the purple fires of Shamar. He believed Earth was sending a spy among their group of exchange students.

"Also, the one known as Dr. Meddars is a seer — a weak one, but he sees," Ishma continued. "He is susceptible to Rube, as is the other human male."

Raggion snarled at Ishma, but didn't call him out for pointing out his lapse in judgement.

"Your idea of a little joke, Raggion?" Lord Halvati demanded. "You will apologize to our guests at the high meal. And if word of this gets back to the council, I will not protect you."

"Rube? A minor prank." Lord Tobul laughed. Tobul was old, but he still had a warrior's body. Muscles developed from years of physical training rippled beneath his robes. The battle wings folded behind him could still carry him aloft for several hours at a time. His bald head had only a single long tuft of hair on top. "I do not approve of humans being brought to Aldebar, but it is my duty to protect and guide them. I will fulfill that duty with honor."

"They will serve the high meal in the captain's dining hall in ten minutes," a voice announced over the ship's communication system. Raggion stood and nodded to the others in the room. Each stood in order of rank, Lord Tobul, the senior member of the council, standing last.

"Let's join our guests. A good meal promotes harmony." Rom Ishma spoke as if he, not Raggion, were the host. Since this was the nature of the Degg, no one, least of all Raggion, took offense.

CHAPTER SEVENTEEN
—Space—Bengari Vessel

Careful design created the illusion of spaciousness in the captain's dining hall. The end walls reflected the interior furnishings with mirror mosaics that contrasted with the long walls of alabaster. A sleek ebony table, elegant in its simplicity, held room for twelve. It surprised Kelli when one of the crew escorted her to this table instead of the round table with the other students.

Kelli admired the design of the table while Duncan and Michael chatted with Shual. The table stood bare. Their host, Captain Raggion, was already fifteen minutes late. The door slid open and Rom Ishma entered, followed by the captain and two ambassadors.

Rom Ishma said, "Greetings, students, doctors. May I present your host, Captain Raggion. We also have the honor of dining with Lord Halvati of the House of Bengar, and Lord Tobul of the House of Shamar." Rom Nebbar made brief introductions.

With eyes lowered, Kelli extended both hands with the palms up to Captain Raggion in what, according to Shual, was a standard Bengari greeting. In response, he laid his hands palms down on hers, pressing down. She looked up, smiling into the surprised face of the captain. The simple greeting had taken practice, but she performed it well. Raggion's smile softened his face. She lowered her head and offered her hands, this time to Lord Halvati. When she felt the responding greeting, she looked up into the violet eyes of Lord Tobul. She was confused. How had he switched places with Lord Halvati?

"A beautiful greeting, my lady." The old Shamaru war lord nodded. His face was impossible to read as he studied her reaction for a moment, and then turned to greet her companions.

Kelli's heart hammered, her eyes glued to Lord Tobul as he greeted Duncan. She could have reached out and touched the gray and white wings folded across his back. If she could get one feather from those wings, she could do the genetic profile in a few hours.

Shual interrupted her thoughts, suggesting that she take a seat. "They are ready to serve us now."

Kelli found herself between Lord Tobol and Rom Ishma. Duncan sat across from her between Shual and Lord Halvati. The captain was at the head of the table, with Michael at his right hand. The guests sat and four ranking officers entered, bowed, and filled the empty places. They were all Bengari.

They served drinks in ceremonial goblets to begin the formal meal. Kelli lifted her goblet, admiring the design etched into the exterior. Its silver glass shone in the light.

When Michael hesitated to drink, Lord Halvati glared at Captain Raggion. The captain hastened to apologize.

"My apologies for not warning you about the effects of Rube. Had I seen Miss Royal, I would have known it was unnecessary. Her beauty is enough to warm the coldest blood. I assure you that this is a mild tea and nothing more."

Something in the captain's tone assured everyone that both the apology and compliment were sincere. So, for the sake of diplomacy, Michael accepted them. "No harm done, Captain, and we took no offense."

Kelli sipped the fruity tea and nodded her head toward

Captain Raggion. "It's quite delicious. What is it called?"

"It is Mavock tea. The Mavock plant grows wild in the Nellar region. The roots are quite poisonous, but the flower makes the best tea in all of Aldebar." What Captain Raggion did not say was how rare the Mavock plant had become in recent years. Lord Halvati's disapproval of the Rube had prompted him to open his private stash of the fine tea.

After removing the drinks, the server placed a small plate with three pear-shaped objects in front of Kelli. A pleasant aroma filled the room. What appeared to be a large platter of loaves of flat bread sat in the center of the table.

"Kopuck is a small sea animal. Roasted, it has a fine flavor. Take one in your hand and peel back the tough skin. Eat it with the bread," Lord Tobol explained as he took one from his plate and demonstrated.

The kopuck turned out to be quite tasty. The meat under the skin was white, juicy, and sweet to the taste. Kelli soon finished the three kopuck, each the size of a small egg, and four of the flat loaves of soft bread. Before she could protest that she was quite full, they replaced her empty plate with one containing another meat. This meat swam in a pungent smelling sauce. The captain ate it with his fingers as if he were eating barbecued ribs. Kelli found the taste less to her liking than kopuck, but not bad.

Duncan was on his second plate of the new meat, which Shual called gonarr, or mountain goat. He held a piece toward Kelli. "Tastes like horseradish sauce."

"You're right, it does," she replied.

Soon the servers placed bowls of warm water with a touch of cleanser before each guest, and small towels across each lap. Kelli followed Captain Raggion's lead, first washing her hands in the bowl, and then drying them on the towel. They removed the towels and bowls and served each guest a goblet of clear green wine.

"High meal always begins with tea to awaken the appetite,

and ends with wine to assure good digestion of the meat," Shual explained. "Unless you're from Deggar. We Degg do not mix wine with food."

Their meal complete, the captain returned to the bridge of his ship and his guests headed to their quarters for some much-needed sleep.

Kelli stopped by to visit Liesel and Rachel before calling it a day. Rachel lay on her bed reading, while Liesel worked on a pastel likeness of the Bengari guards who had welcomed them on board the ship.

"That's excellent, Liesel. I sat next to Captain Raggion at supper, and I think you captured the skin tones and facial features."

Liesel screwed her face up. "As close as I could. Pastel is not my best medium, and far from my favorite. I'm finishing this up and putting things away now."

"Good idea. Dr. Gentry wants to meet with us before breakfast in the morning."

Kelli stepped out and into the long corridor. Her next stop was Marla and Ammie's room. She found the girls getting ready to go out. They were chatting as they put on makeup.

"What's going on?" Kelli asked. She knew of nowhere the girls could go on board the vessel.

"Ammie met this Bengari cadet, Rommel, at supper—I mean high meal—and he invited us to the ship's lounge to hear him play in a band." Marla hastened to give an explanation.

"And you agreed without checking with one of the team leaders first?" Kelli's disapproval sounded in her voice.

"We didn't have to ask permission to go out at Barringer's, as long as we were back before curfew," Marla protested

"They cooped us up on the shuttle a long time. We're young, and we need to have a little fun." Ammie whined and her lower lip poked out with disappointment.

"I'll talk to Shual, and if he says this won't create a problem,

I'll accompany you to the lounge."

"Thanks," Marla exclaimed.

Kelli headed toward Shual's room at the far end of the hall. She pushed the buzzer and identified herself. The door slid open and Shual, clad in a silver robe, bowed.

"Come in, Miss Royal...Kelli."

The fragrance of incense filled the air. Kelli saw candles and what looked like dried leaves burning on a small alter. "I've interrupted your meditations. Please forgive me."

Shual stepped aside. "You honor this one with your presence. How may I serve you?

"I need your advice. A crewman invited Ammie and Marla to the ship's lounge. I don't know if this is proper. We wouldn't want to offend anyone, or to give the crew members the wrong idea. We know little about your cultures, and are young and impulsive."

"I don't think it would offend anyone, but it is not usual for adolescent females to go to the lounge unchaperoned. The crew might not treat you with the respect the captain wishes his guests to receive. With your permission, I will escort your party to the lounge."

"That is very kind, Shual." Kellie gave him a grateful smile. Their brief encounters had somehow sparked in her an affinity for Rom Ishma's assistant. Behind his quiet, ethereal exterior, Kelli sensed in the Degg representative a quick mind and lively personality. She would enjoy seeing Shual in a less formal setting.

Later, seated at a small table in the crowded lounge, Kelli noted that their presence created a stir. She was thankful that Shual had accompanied them. More eyes watched them than the band playing on stage. Kelli was watching the Bengari soldiers. Shual seemed calm and was enjoying the music. Deciding to relax, Kelli found she enjoyed the music's soothing sound. It almost reminded her of Middle Eastern folk music.

Marla and Ammie watched the tall, handsome Bengari cadet, enrapt. His behavior had become very formal when Shual and Kelli greeted him at the door. After a few moments of awkward introduction, he asked Ammie and Marla to join his table to watch the next group perform. Kelli smiled and nodded. She could use the time to talk to Shual alone.

"Lord Tobol isn't Bengari. What does the term House of Shamar mean?" Kelli began questioning, nothing that wouldn't pass for normal curiosity.

"That is a political designation which refers to the ruling class in the Shamaru Homeland. There are ruling houses in all the homelands on Aldebar. Shamar is a high mountainous country. They build cities into the sides of cliffs and on top of mountain peaks. In ancient days, the Shamaru flew down from their cities and raided the lower lands. They were fierce warriors."

"His wingspan looked enormous. Are they still functional?"

"Yes, a Shamaru in good health can stay in flight for hours. Inside their homeland, they prefer their wings to any other means of transportation." Shual seemed to enjoy his role as instructor in Aldebarian culture.

"Is the city of Rishal in the Shamaru homeland?"

"No, Rishal is an open city in my homeland of Deggar, near the Bengari boarder. There are many Shamaru who live and trade in Rishal. Our scientific products are popular exports throughout Aldebar."

Kelli wasn't sure what an open city was. Her background information was thin. Her mind flittered back to the training film from the Space Center. All she could remember was that it had something to do with trade. Shual saw her confusion and explained what she was to learn was one foundation of Aldebarian society.

"One can see it confuses you. Perhaps this one can explain without too great a burden of history. After the Great Wars, they gave each of the seven sentient peoples a homeland.

They established three large trading cities in each homeland. These cities are open to all peoples, but they restrict access to the interior of the homelands to the people of that land. Some peoples enforce their border laws more than others, but no one violates the border of another people."

Kelli's mind kicked into top gear. How far in the past were the Great Wars? Was there any remaining hostility on Aldebar? Her experiences with UNWL made her suspect they might send her into danger. She studied the blue-green liquid in her glass, trying to summon the courage to question Shual about the political environment on Aldebar.

"Are you troubled about something, Miss Royal?" Shual had picked up on the silent body language that was signaling her thoughts.

"I'm tired," Kelli answered, realizing there was greater safety in keeping her eyes open and her mouth shut.

"You don't trust me," Shual responded.

"Are all Degg so perceptive?" Kelli said.

"No, you're a very poor liar."

Taken back by such an unusual response, Kelli answered, "Sorry."

"Don't be, it takes practice to be a good liar. This one can sense you are an honest person."

"Sometimes honesty can be a dangerous thing," Kelli responded, chaffing at the knowledge that her entire identity was one big lie. Like father, like son, they say, or in this case, daughter.

"Still, it is a quality this one prizes in a friend," Shual said.

"Are you a friend?" The wistful tone in Kelli's voice made it sound like a plea.

"Of a kind. They sent this one to find out about the virus that disabled your shuttle."

"But you were at the space station waiting." Kelli's voice rose with emotion. Shual motioned for her to lower her voice. She did, but couldn't hide her emotion. "That means you knew about the virus weeks in advance." Then, as the reality sank deeper into her mind, she continued in a whisper, "The virus didn't originate on Earth."

"When we learned about the virus, it was too late to call off the mission. They sent me to rescue the shuttle and track the virus back to the source." Shual shook his head. "When you destroyed the virus, we lost the information needed to trace the source."

"Maybe not." Kelli ran tired fingers across her forehead. "You scanned the shuttle's com system?"

"Extensively—no trace of the virus or the program that purged it," Shual answered, adding, "It's odd not to find even the smallest trace of a program."

"It is odd, but not impossible for a program to be untraceable." A hint of smugness filtered into Kelli's voice. It gratified her to learn that the Aldebarian considered her work advanced.

"Perhaps if one understood such a program, one could retrieve the information needed to trace the virus."

"Perhaps, if you had the shuttle's program," Kelli responded. Shual was close to uncovering Eric.

"We downloaded the shuttle's program and made a spectra copy." Shual reached out a silvery hand and placed it on top of Kelli's. "If we don't find out who planted that virus, they will try again to sabotage this project."

"Are you sure I can help you?" Kelli countered, wishing that Michael and Duncan were in on this discussion.

"One is not sure of anything. But if correct, this belongs to you." Reaching into the pocket of his flowing black robe, Shual produced a small star-shaped chip wrapped in a clear packing bubble. Kelli had never even seen a program chip shaped like that before, and said so. Shual turned it in his hand, and then she detected the faintest blue flicker. Attached to the program chip was the tiny linker she had sent out. She paled, not saying a word. She didn't have to.

"It was you." Shual's head bounced up and down with excitement. "When we ruled out your UNWL as the source of this, I knew that whoever sent it would be aboard the shuttle."

"How long have you known about the linker?" Kelli dropped all pretense.

"It was located a few days after the exchange program went into full operation, about nine Earth months ago." Shual sounded quite pleased with himself. He noticed the corners of Kelli's mouth turn up into a smile. He no longer looked quite so pleased. "How long did you have it operational before we located it?"

"Almost two years, give or take a week or two. It depends on the exact date you found it."

Shual muttered something that came over the translator as garble. Kelli waited for the translator to change the word into Barric and then English, but it never did.

"You wanted honesty," Kelli responded. "If the UNWL had been up to something underhanded, I would have warned you. The link works both ways."

"You would have betrayed your own government." Shual seemed aghast.

"I don't trust my government," Kelli answered. "Are you sure you can trust yours?

"No." Shual sighed. "The House of Deggar is, of course, trustworthy, but slow to act. Events have pulled the Council of Unity in a hundred directions. Power swapping back and forth between lords. It is dangerous to deal with the council. One must look over one's shoulder to protect one's back."

"Of course," Kelli echoed.

"You will help, won't you?" Shual asked. Both were eager to finish their discussion before Ammie and Marla returned to the table.

"I'll talk to Professor Gentry. We can meet with you and

Rom Ishma in the morning."

"My Rom doesn't know about this. He sees this one as a new aide assigned to him by the high lord."

They agreed to a meeting the next day. The girls returned and Kelli went with them back to their rooms to sleep. Kelli saw no reason to disturb Michael's rest.

Sleep, what a wonderful thing, Kelli thought as she tossed in the comfortable sleep tube. It refreshed the body and cleared the mind. She willed herself to sleep, without success. After an hour of trying, Kelli dug into the team's first aid case and took a mild sedative. It worked, and she drifted into a dream world of mazes. She ran first this way and then the other, getting further into the maze but no closer to an exit. Somehow panic drove her forward, but she couldn't remember if she were running from some danger or trying to reach something in time. *In time for what?* The dream held her like a whirlpool, spinning and pulling down, down, down.

The wake-up alarm jerked her from the dream. Kelli fought through the sedative haze to shut it off. The face in the mirror looked tired, hollow-eyed, and fearful. Her pupils shone large in her eyes. Kelli washed her face and neck using the chilled drinking water. The icy shock had the desired effect. Her head cleared; all traces of grogginess gone.

It surprised Michael to see her up and about so early. Kelli had sent a message that she was going with Ammie and Marla to the ship's lounge, and he had a vague idea how late they had turned in. He had showered, shaved, and was buttoning the sleeves on a clean white shirt. Kelli's rumpled, tired appearance amused him. "You can't let them keep you out so late and get up this early. Go back to bed for a few hours. You look like a zombie."

"I wish I could." Kelli sighed. "Shual wants a private meeting with you, me, and Duncan as soon as possible. Let's grab Duncan and I'll brief you both before breakfast."

Duncan did not answer his door. After several buzzes, the door slid open. Duncan stood there wrapped in a thick black terry robe, rubbing his hair dry. His voice sounded deep and raspy.

"Good morning. To what do I owe the honor of this wake-up call?" He smiled and stepped aside, motioning for them to come in.

"I hope it is a good morning," Kelli began. "Shual and I talked in the ship's lounge last night. If what he says is true, the virus that disabled our shuttle originated on Aldebar, not Earth."

"That makes little sense. How could a virus get from Aldebar into our shuttle's computer?" Michael voiced his doubt. The problem with his logic was that it was limited by his knowledge of Earth's government-controlled technology.

"It's not that complicated. Stick a virus on a linker chip, patch it on a communication, and bingo. The complicated part would be to devise some sort of homing trigger so the virus affects the shuttle's computer and not the Bengari vessel."

"Or if, as Kelli's existence suggests, Aldebar has already had covert agents on Earth, an operative could have set it there."

Duncan voiced a fear playing in her mind. Before that possibility could be discussed, Shual entered. He was shaking and sounded distraught. A bad morning got worse.

"This one has failed. Oh, such shame and dishonor are mine," Shual sobbed, "One underestimated enemies, and our children have paid the price for my failure."

"Calm down. What about the students?" Michael's voice commanded an answer. Gone was his usual calm. He kept enough control to stop himself from grabbing the Degg and shaking him.

"Not your students. They have destroyed the shuttle carrying the students from Aldebar. The news will come over the intercom."

Shock settled over the small group. Kelli went to Shual, wrapping her arms around his thin shoulders, the silence and his pain cutting through her like a knife. She could find no words to help him. The silence grew.

Shual composed himself enough to warn them to stay in their quarters and to make sure the other students didn't wander around the ship. He promised to send food and come back when he had more news.

"Gather all the students in my room. It's the largest." Michael was calmer now. "Once they're all safe and accounted for, meet back here. Try not to scare them."

"Oh right, I'm terrified. I'm locking them all in one room and I'm not supposed to scare them. How do I manage that?" Kelli's frustration spilled over in the sarcastic remark.

"You're a genius, you'll think of something," Michael answered. His smile said that he understood. They were under strain. She would do her best. They would all do their best.

Kelli and Duncan left then to gather the students.

***

Alone, Michael bowed his head. He prayed for the courage and wisdom to protect and to lead those depending on his ability. Their lives and the lives of those lost on the shuttle were heavy on his shoulders.

CHAPTER EIGHTEEN
—SPACE—BENGARI VESSEL

Anger and depression settled over the ship like a tremendous storm threatening to spew forth a deluge of violent retribution. The resentment and suspicion boring into Kelli were palpable as she passed down the corridors of the ship. She was thankful for Shual's presence as she went back to her room.

"Bengari are a proud people," Shual explained, "The crew takes it as an affront to their honor that the students have died so soon after leaving their care."

Captain Raggion was no longer civil to the Earth team. He ranted and raved about being ordered to abandon the investigation after three days and proceed back to Aldebar, and said that they had brought a black mark on his service record, one that would carry to the end of his career. No amount of reasoning could soften his opinion, The crew shared his view. In all, eight students and four professors had perished. Kelli shuddered at the thought of facing their parents on Aldebar.

Communications with Earth had been troubling. They were investigating the disaster, but so far had found nothing. Whether the Aldebar Project would proceed or end before they reached Aldebar was in Michael Gentry's hands. The UNWL authorities pressured him to go ahead, the success of the program being their chief concern. Kelli avoided talking to Michael for three days, feeling that she might influence his decision, and knowing in her heart that she would never get another chance to find out about her heritage, her father, and the reasons for the lie he had lived.

Forced by the imminent departure of the Bengari vessel, Michael called a leadership meeting. He had reached a decision.

Kelli entered the small conference room, surprised that she was the last to arrive. She was even more surprised to see Shual there. Since she was in fact a few minutes early, there was no reason to apologize for keeping them waiting. Kelli took the seat next to Duncan.

"I have invited Shual to join us to represent Aldebarian interests, and because I have leaned on his understanding and knowledge to make my decision to continue on to Aldebar." Michael announced his decision first.

"Are you sure it's safe to continue?" Duncan asked.

"It's as safe as returning to Earth. There are no guarantees that the virus hasn't infected every shuttle in the UNWL fleet. The Bengari vessel seems to function in top form. The captain ran a full diagnostic sweep of the ship's computer."

"We may not be safe if we stay aboard and proceed to Aldebar," Kelli cautioned. "I'm not so sure that a diagnostic sweep would detect a cognizant virus."

"You're right, and we already know that the virus originated on Aldebar, not Earth." Michael looked into her eyes adding, "Shual assures me that whoever destroyed the shuttle will try again."

"But why? How could a group of exchange students threaten anyone? Why would they kill to stop the program?"

"That, Miss Royal, is the question this one must answer. Why one requires your help to trace the virus, and the help of your cognizant program," Shual answered.

Kelli stared at Michael. The least he could have done was

to warn her he was telling the Aldebarians about Eric. He knew the problem with Eric's primary function was still there.

"Kelli, you will work with Shual to find out as much as possible about that virus. We know we are going into a hostile environment. We will use every resource available to us to protect the students and aide the Aldebarians in tracking down whoever caused the deaths aboard the Earth shuttle."

There were nods of agreement. Kelli applauded the wisdom of Michael's words. The old saying "When the going gets tough, the tough get going" came to her mind. The weight of leadership was heavy on his shoulders, but he bore it well.

"Duncan, it's hard for me to admit when I'm wrong. I've been unfair to you. We don't understand your abilities, and maybe I feared them a little. It was wrong of me to forbid you to use them. You're released from that promise, and I apologize for my stupidity. We will need you, and perhaps those abilities, to sort this mess out."

Duncan held out his hand to Michael, pledging his total support. They discussed his psychic talents. "My abilities are mediocre. Sometimes I can read thoughts and powerful emotions. I get readings from people, but I can't see the future. Some psychics can visit a murder scene and get a picture so accurate the police can use it to catch the murderer. I'm nowhere near that level."

"Duncan's being too modest. He's pioneering research in mind-link. If what I've read is correct, he can not only read thoughts, but he can send messages telepathically. He used that talent to reach into the mind of a child and pull the child back to reality in three sessions." Kelli had downloaded a copy of Duncan's published research papers from the library at Canaveral Space Center. Those papers had made interesting reading during the voyage to Space Station Alpha Three.

Duncan smiled, flattered that she had studied his work. "Gifted students often score high on the psychic abilities scale, but no one understands why."

Michael directed attention back to their problem by asking Shual, "How far can we trust the Aldebarian government?"

"You can trust me. Degg are incapable of dishonesty, and several of the students who died were from Deggar. I will reveal nothing we discuss here to anyone outside this room. My concern is to identify and capture those responsible for the deaths aboard the shuttle."

Michael nodded, his eyes narrowing, a sign that he had not missed the implications of Shual's response.

Kelli knew Shual had given an honest answer, one that revealed as much about his character as it did about the trustworthiness of the Aldebarian governments. She glanced at Michael and then replied, "Anything you reveal in confidence will remain in this room. The UNWL can get their own information."

Later, after the others had gone and they were alone in the briefing room, Kelli spent a few minutes explaining to Shual about the cognizant program, and what its programing was on this trip. She also remembered that the Eric program had identified the virus as a cognizant chip, or in this case the Aldebarian equivalent.

"whoot...." Shual uttered an owl-like sound, almost a cry of distress. If the Degg possessed such technology, his sense of honor refused to consider that his own people were responsible for such a heinous crime. Several students and professors on the shuttle had been from the Degg Homeland.

"If one eliminates the Degg as a possibility, three sources of the advanced technology remain. We can rule out the Bengari or Shamaru. They fight their enemies face to face, and see dishonor in such senseless sabotage. A group of Narr had to be behind this. Proving that to the Council of Unity will be difficult, the Narr being such powerful members of the council."

"What is it, Shual?" Kelli asked. She could tell he was onto something.

"My enemy may be more powerful than imagined." Shual rubbed his silver hands together as if to warm away the icy fear he was feeling.

"Our enemy," Kelli said, and gripped his silvery hands with her warm human ones. He responded to their warmth. Kelli realized with a start that the Degg were not warm-blooded creatures.

"Our enemy," Shual continued. "Let's start by seeing how much information we can retrieve with your program."

Shual, under other circumstances, might have been excited to study such advanced alien technology. They reported technology far more advanced than Earth claimed to possess.

"We need a self-contained database and com station. My partner programmed Eric to function as my personal bodyguard — his idea of a goodbye present. I don't want to endanger this vessel by giving it access to the ship's control network."

"The program will only activate if you are in danger?" Shual asked.

"Someone has already tried to blow up one shuttle I was on. That activated the function," Kelli explained, "That's why I shut Eric down."

"What does Eric mean?"

"Nothing, it's his name."

"You name your machines?"

"Yes, and hurricanes too," Duncan explained, grinning, "It's an old Earth custom."

"Hurricanes?" Then as the delayed translation found a suitable Aldebarian definition, Shual continued. "Windstorms. Yes, I am familiar with those, but we do not name our atmospheric disturbances on Aldebar."

Shual programmed a shield that he felt would block Eric's access to the ship's control functions, and still allow for maximum use of the cognizant. In minutes, light patterns flickered across the screen. The hologram of Eric stood on the com-panel.

"I am in an unknown system. Please wait, I am attempting to identify. Please wait while I adjust processing codes and memory. Visual and vocal identification online, please give voice input."

"Voice command Kelli One, Eric. Sorry to leave you so long."

"Processing.... Voice identification complete. Please identify non-human in program sector."

"This is my Aldebarian friend, Shual. We must help him locate the source of the virus you destroyed on the shuttle."

"Processing.... The virus was not of Earth design." The hologram appeared in front of Shual.

"I know that. We need everything your memory retained from that encounter. Shual will go over it. He will also give you access to certain databases. He has authorization for full use of your functions."

"Please give voice pattern for security lock," the holographic program instructed.

Kelli nodded, and Shual stated his name and rank. Soon she had cleared Shual to access all of Eric's functions. It produced a printout in perfect Deggarian script. It amazed Shual.

"That's what makes Eric unique. He is capable of independent cognizant functioning," Kelli said, then added, "Eric, could I have a copy in English, please?"

Days of study seemed to confirm Shual's suspicions about the Narr. Not enough evidence to implicate the Narr government, but more than enough to warn the proper members of the High Council. They sent a coded message, and the rest of the voyage they used to prepare the students for the culture in Rishal.

CHAPTER NINETEEN
—Aldebar Prime—Degg Homeland

The following morning, Kelli was opening the door to her room when she heard voices and recognized Michael Gentry talking to Captain Raggion. She shut the door but left it open a crack to listen. The captain might not want to talk in the presence of a student.

"News of the tragedy has reached Aldebar. That may lead to demonstrations protesting the humans. We will land under cover of darkness. They will change our time and landing site for security reasons," Raggion said.

"Thank you for keeping me updated, Captain. I can understand this has created an unpleasant situation," Michael Gentry replied.

The captain's voice lowered. "Rom Ishma and his aide have convinced me that your government was not responsible for the tragedy. We must look closer to home to find the enemies who did this."

Kelli stepped back as the two men passed her door. Neither seemed to have noticed the small opening. She breathed a sigh of relief.

***

The captain awoke the passengers in the middle of their

sleep in time to disembark. Kelli was sleepy and irritated that things kept changing. She moved up to walk beside Shual. He was silent until two worker Degg met them. Rom Ishma introduced them as the high lord of Deggar and the head of Rishal's open school. Security adequate for riot control lined the area. Shual remained silent and tense as Rom Ishma made introductions, but Kelli was close enough to see his trembling.

"What's wrong?" Kelli whispered as they walked toward the transport.

"This one is without knowledge of the matter. It does not feel right. This is neither the time nor place Lord Ravon had planned for our return. We could not stop the Narr from destroying the shuttle, and the high lord of Deggar requires an explanation for my failure."

"He can't blame you. You had no way to know the virus infected the other shuttle."

Shual lowered his head, weighed down by guilt. "You are kind, but they sent this one to ensure this exchange was safe, and I have failed. Aldebarian students died because of that failure."

"You weren't responsible for the shuttle explosion; you did all you could to ensure the safety of all our students." Kelli reached out and squeezed the silvery hand. "Quit blaming yourself, Rema."

To use his sacred name without permission was a breach of Deggarian etiquette. The Degg reserved that for the most intimate of situations or relationships. She hoped he could sense the genuine concern and compassion she felt, and forgive the unintentional transgression.

"One will try, friend," Shual replied, but his voice lacked conviction.

***

Though the students were eager to see Rishal, they only glimpsed its side roads as the transport sped through the city. The sun was setting as they arrived at a large gray building with an arched entrance and domed roof. Kelli could make out the Deggarian symbol of knowledge, a two-headed bird in flight, etched above the entrance. It was a sacred hall of knowledge and wisdom.

The students and staff of the open school had gathered to welcome them. They seemed eager to meet the visitors from Earth and welcome them to Rishal.

Rom Nashi, head of the Deggarian school, spoke. "Welcome, brothers and sisters from Earth. Here you will meet students from all the homelands except the Darro. Narr students will join us for the first time. This is a momentous time indeed."

A moment of fear coursed through Kelli. Wasn't Shual sure that the Narr had something to do with the shuttle's destruction? She willed herself to relax and recognized the tall catlike Bengari, the silver skinned Degg, and the winged Shamaru among the students. From Shual's descriptions, she could identify the tall apelike students as members of the Gelt homeland. He had told her that the school boasted students from five of the seven Homelands of Aldebar. Seeing them standing together struck Kelli more by their similarities than the obvious differences. "They're all humanoid bipeds."

"The creator made all sentient peoples in his image," Shual responded to Kelli's surprised observation. "We also find this written in your holy book. We confirmed this truth when our worlds met."

Before that statement could sink in, Rom Ishma pulled Kelli away and introduced her to the faculty of the Deggarian Open School. Rom Nashi, the school's director, was an older Degg who moved with stiffness from guest to guest, greeting each with a traditional Earth handshake. The gesture touched Kelli.

"Rom Ishma tells me you are indeed an extraordinary young woman, Miss Royal. I shall enjoy working with you." Rom Nashi gave her hand an extra squeeze.

"I'm so sorry about your people," Kelli began, realizing

that Rom Nashi must have known and selected each student and professor who had died aboard the shuttle. No words could express how he must feel.

"Let this sorrow bring our worlds together, Miss Royal. That will honor their memory."

Kelli sensed that someone was watching her. She felt hostility. Turning her head, she locked eyes with a tall Shamaru wearing a beautiful turquoise robe. He said something to Shual, and headed across the room toward her. If her instincts were correct, she was about to meet Lord Ravon, who oversaw the exchange.

"Rom Nashi, I would like a word with our guest, if you don't mind." Lord Ravon's words were courteous enough, but there was an edge to his voice.

Rom Nashi sighed, his mouth opening quavering. There was no escaping the censorious tone in his voice when he spoke. "I see you have not yet achieved patience, young lord. Does not our guest deserve some refreshments and a night's rest before you interrogate her?"

"It's all right, Rom Nashi. If I can help Lord Ravon, I will be more than happy to speak with him as soon as possible," Kelli replied. She extended her hands in Aldebarian fashion to Lord Ravon, who remembered his manners and returned the greeting.

Shual came to stand behind Kelli, and she felt his silvery hand rest on her shoulder.

"I have explained to Lord Ravon that without your efforts no one would have survived, and we would lose any hope of tracing the source of the virus." Shual inserted himself as a buffer between Kelli and Lord Ravon.

Rom Nashi alerted Michael, and he joined Shual at her side. "Thank you, Shual. I'm sure Lord Ravon understands my student needs rest and will be available at the debriefing in the morning."

"I'm not tired, and I'm sure Lord Ravon won't mind

discussing business over dinner. It's an old Earth custom." Kelli nodded for Shual to go. He hesitated for a moment, then turned and went to join Rom Nashi. Michael stood firm at her side, matching Lord Ravon's look, glare for glare.

"Professor Gentry is correct. Tomorrow will be soon enough to discuss the shuttle tragedy. It would honor me, however, to escort you to the dining hall for the high meal," Lord Ravon agreed and offered her his arm. The silver wings folded across his back formed a velvety feather cape, with the tips brushing the floor. "If that is permitted by your many protectors."

Together they walked into the dining hall under the watchful eyes of Shual and Michael. They had prepared a special meal for the guests from Earth. After cups of spicy tea, they placed platters of assorted meats and breads on each table. Kelli had become accustomed to Aldebarian dining on the journey aboard the Bengari vessel. Breakfast was comprised of breads and fruit or cooked grains with lots of steaming goat's milk. This strong milk was not popular with the Earth students. About midmorning, they enjoyed a second meal, an informal buffet of exotic Aldebarian fruits and vegetables, sweet pastries, and a sour drink, which was sweetened by holding sweet crystals in the mouth while sipping it. The third meal was always hot soup or stew and more sweet pastries. The high meal was the most important meal of the day. It was a formal banquet of meats, breads, and wine.

Everyone enjoyed the meal as they got to know the students and faculty of the open school. Lord Ravon was true to his word and kept the conversation light. There was no mention of computer sabotage, spies, or death. Rom Nashi showed the weary travelers to their new quarters and bid them a good night's sleep.

Kelli leaned against the door to what was to be her room for the next three years. Someone had delivered her personal things from the Bengari vessel, and she put them away in the drawers built into one wall. They built everything into the walls. One wall housed a library from ceiling to floor. A workstation and terminal were in another wall. Its comfortable chair appeared to be the only furniture not attached or built in. Kelli found the bed; tripped over the bed might be a more accurate description. They had recessed it into the floor so she had to get down on the floor to get into bed. Once she got in, it was beyond anything she had ever imagined. Her body floated on a mattress of warm gasses as gentle pulses along her back lulled her to sleep, a deep REM sleep. She learned at breakfast the next morning that Degg sleep experts designed these beds to make sleeping more efficient and cut down on the rest time required by their users.

***

Their debriefing with Lord Ravon and the Deggarian high lord began with the calm and formality of Deggarian custom, but grew tense.

"The Council of Unity had to act. Rumors of spies and assassins among your team are rampant throughout many of the homelands. I have been ordered to investigate this linker chip. Pending the outcome of that probe, we must restrict your activity to the school campus and monitor your computer activity," said Lord Ravon. He shot Kelli a look to show whose computer activity was of primary concern.

"That's crazy. Why would we try to destroy a shuttle and kill ourselves?" Michael raised his voice in exasperation.

"No one here is accusing you, Professor Gentry," the high lord of Deggar replied. The look on Lord Ravon's face said he was giving no such assurances.

"And well you shouldn't. You knew about the danger and failed to warn Earth. We could have all died." Kelli went on the offensive. "How will the council explain that bit of information?"

"What does that mean, Miss Royal? It sounds like a threat." Lord Ravon's voice was razor sharp, and his violet eyes danced with rage.

"It means you know bloody well that we had nothing to do with the destruction of that shuttle, and we're not taking the blame for it, and neither is Shual." Kelli almost demanded to know where Shual was. They must have interrogated him about the shuttle and failing his mission. Perhaps he was being punished or made Lord Ravon's scapegoat. Her lavender eyes met Lord Ravon's fire for fire.

"Dr. Gentry, I suggest you control your student," Lord Ravon said.

"Try it yourself; I think you'll find it's an impossible task," Michael replied good-naturedly. Remaining calm while Lord Ravon was fuming gave him a decided advantage.

A psychic vision mellowed Duncan. In a rich baritone voice, he said, "Ravon knows who sabotaged the shuttle. What he knows frightens him."

Lord Ravon moved to strike out at Duncan, but the silvery hand of the high lord grabbed his arm. "Would you dare dishonor a seer, Ravon? He is one that speaks the truth."

Lord Ravon turned an abashed face toward Duncan and apologized. "We esteem seers in the Shamaru homeland, and to raise my hand in anger at even an alien seer is a terrible offense. Forgive me, Man of Sight; I lost control of my temper."

"A trait you share with my student, Lord Ravon." Duncan's calm voice and unruffled manner seemed to sooth Lord Ravon, and the tension eased in the room. Lord Ravon apologized again and explained that without proof he could not accuse a member of the High Council with such a crime.

"We will do everything we can to help you apprehend whoever is guilty, Lord Ravon. We do not wish them to destroy our mission." Michael reached out in a conciliatory manner.

Kelli found the Shamaru lord arrogant, even frightening, but sensed he would make a better ally than an enemy.

***

Lord Ravon found the earth professor stuffy and

perplexing. Professor Gentry exuded an aura of quiet authority, yet he had allowed his female student to answer his challenge. Lord Ravon had faced enough men in battle and across the council room to recognize bravery, and would have chosen this man to be at his side in either. Did this earth man not deem Lord Ravon of Shamaru worthy of his personal attention?

That earth girl was as fiery as a Nellari witch, and almost as beautiful. Perhaps she had the same power to enslave a man, and Dr. Gentry was under her spell. His own leader, Lord Travalla, had defied the High Council and married a Nellari princess. To this day she remained his wife, as was the Shamaru custom. Lord Ravon watched Kelli. Shual seemed smitten with this Earth female too, and not even a Nellari witch had the power to charm a Degg.

"We welcome your help, Dr. Gentry." The high lord nudged Lord Ravon, and Lord Ravon took the hand Michael offered. It was a crude facsimile of a handshake, Lord Ravon not being used to relinquishing control of his fighting hand, but he found he could measure the strength of a man by this Earth custom. A bond formed between strangers by the touch.

***

Later Kelli, Michael, and Duncan met with the students and tried to calm their fears. They had picked up on the tension and were full of questions.

"Are we going back to Earth? Are we safe here?" Peter asked. "We've been watching some protests on their communications network."

Michael cleared his throat. "We have no plans to return to Earth. The High Council has assured me we are safe. They will clear up this misunderstanding soon, and we will continue our original mission."

"But I'm afraid," said Marla. "If the Aldebarians don't want us here, I think we should go home."

Kelli put an arm around the shaking girl. "We're in an

unfamiliar environment, and it is natural to experience anxiety after what happened on the voyage. The High Council is doing everything it can to ensure our safety. I think we should stay calm, begin our studies, and let them worry about security."

That afternoon afforded Kelli a golden opportunity. She was observing a class in the school's impressive science laboratory when the professor displayed a new biogenic station. The students were studying inherited characteristics. She had used a more rudimentary station at Barringer's, where the students checked each other for inherited diseases.

After class, she was alone in the lab. Kelli activated the station. She would run a scan on her own blood sample. Kelli pricked her finger and squeezed the drops needed for the test strip. The station hummed, and in minutes a printout appeared in the tray. Kelli stared at the results, unable to read a word of the Deggarian script. She folded the printout and tucked it into an empty pocket.

"Miss Royal, Rom Nashi said I might find you here." Shual's voice startled her. She jumped and stepped away from the biogenic station.

"Shual, you scared me," Kelli chided, then took a more casual tone. "I've been checking out this lab, it's impressive."

"Yes, this is a recent improvement, a gift from a former student," Shual replied, and ducked his head.

Kelli nodded and remarked, "A very wealthy former student."

"When one has the means, one shares," Shual said

As she regained her composure, Kelli's heart rate slowed. She smiled at Shual. "How did your meeting with the High Council go?"

"Not well. They blamed Lord Ravon for not canceling the mission. The Narr lords wanted him stripped of his seat on the council and disgraced." Shual shook his head, as if that would release the troublesome memory. "I thought they had succeeded, but the high lord of Deggar persuaded them that Lord Ravon wasn't responsible."

"Shual, that's wonderful news. Now Lord Ravon doesn't have to worry, and we can find out who was behind that virus."

"I'm afraid it is not so good for you. News of your linker chip has reached the council, and you are now a prime suspect. How anyone on the council got that information we can speculate, but not prove. This one was meticulous when communicating with the high lord of Deggar, and — "

"Everyone knows the Degg are honorable, it's an inbred quality," Kelli teased. "It's not your fault, Shual. What can I do to appease the High Council?"

"This is not a humorous situation, Miss Royal. The High Council is the supreme authority on Aldebar."

"I wasn't trying to be funny, Shual, I don't understand how the council blames me for a virus sent from Aldebar to destroy a space shuttle I was on."

"What were you trying to find out with the linker chip?" The question came out in the same soothing tone that characterized all Deggarian speech.

Kelli cursed that benign melodic sound. She knew Shual would ask and had planned her answer. Over the years of avoiding the UNWL, she had become an expert at deception. Lying to a Degg was next to impossible, especially one who has become your friend. "I was trying to find out about the earlier missions to Earth. There were earlier missions, weren't there? I need to know."

"I am not at liberty to discuss that." Was there a hint of sadness or disappointment in Shual's voice? "You are working for your government then?"

"No, I am not working for the UNWL. I told you that before. Shual, twenty-three years ago, there was another Earth mission. I believe my father was part of that mission." There was no response; Shual seemed to become a frozen statue. Kelli thrust the printout into his hands. "I ran a test on my blood. You can read it. You can translate it for me now. That is why I came."

Kelli stood rubbing her hands together to keep them from shaking while Shual read the printout and then read it again. It was impossible to tell what he was thinking.

"One knows little about the previous missions to Earth, but contact with the inhabitants of the planet would have violated the laws of exploration set forth by the High Council," Shual began.

"What does this test say?" It was easy to get frustrated by Shual's slow, calm reasoning. Kelli repressed the desire to snatch back the printout and race to her room to translate it.

"These results are inconclusive. Without further tests, there is no way to prove that your father was Aldebarian."

"But this supports that possibility, doesn't it?" Kelli couldn't contain the excitement she felt.

"There is an 90% probability that your father was a Creed. That's a hybrid formed when members of different sentient species reproduce. What his ancestry was is harder to speculate on, though from the partial DNA pattern and your eyes I might assume a Shamaru heritage."

"Then you believe me," Kelli said, relieved.

"It isn't necessary for me to believe you. You must convince the Council of Unity," Shual replied.

"But I need you to help me do that. I can't access information about that time, but you could."

"If this one does not help, you will try it yourself regardless of the danger." Shual rationalized his decision. "One can give you information related to your ancestry, and you have to promise to keep a low profile. Don't talk about this with anyone, and keep Eric offline. Your terminal use is being monitored."

"Great, I might as well be back on Earth. Are you sure the Great Council isn't part of the UNWL?"

"We base the Aldebarian government systems on hereditary homelands. There are few similarities with your democratic governments."

"So maybe we should abolish both governments." The contempt in Kelli's voice was long seated. The trauma she had endured at the hands of the UNWL left her with a foundation of fear, and working as an info-raider had honed it well.

"You are very disrespectful of your government, Ms. Royal, yet you represent it."

"Sometimes a government does things that cause it to lose respect." Kelli struggled to find the words to express how she felt and why. She gave up. "It would take too long to explain. It's time for the third meal. Can you join us?"

"No, this one has a great deal of work to complete." Shual placed a hand on her head in parting, a sign of friendship in Deggar. He headed toward the door and stopped. He retrieved the stone of tranquility from his robe. Shual held it out, and when she took the stone, he closed her hand around it and pressed it to her forehead. "The stone will bring inner peace. Keep it near you."

"Thanks." Kelli appreciated the honor of Shual's gift. He had said that peace stones were rare and precious. She looked down. The beautiful blue stone had turned a mesh of purple and orange. "It's not blue, it's—"

"You must bring back its true color," Shual answered.

"How? I know nothing about these stones." Kelli looked at the egg-shaped stone in her palm. The discordant colors screamed at her.

"Hold the stone close to you and remember the blue. The stone will reflect your inner spirit." Shual bowed. "This stone has served me well and will be hard to replace. Keep it close. The orange fighting the purple. In my culture purple is the color of honor, but orange represents pain." Shual shook his head as he looked at the orange. "You have endured much pain for one so young."

CHAPTER TWENTY
—Aldebar Prime—Degg Homeland

A murmur of surprise rippled across the classroom. Interruptions were almost unheard of in Deggarian schools, yet Kelli's class was being interrupted and they were being dismissed. Kelli stood and followed as each student approached the teacher to offer their thanks for the knowledge she had shared with them. It was an old Deggarian custom, one that Kelli found charming.

It amazed her that the different sentient beings could interact with civility. Many of their ancestors had been blood enemies.

The message from Shual said to come to the director's office. Kelli followed the last student down the hall. Michael, Duncan, and Shual were waiting in the office.

"Greetings, Miss Royal. Thank you for your promptness." Shual extended his silvery hands.

"Greetings, Shual. How are we faring with the council?" Kelli was trusting Shual as a friend and advisor. And given the vicious rumors blaming her for the shuttle explosion, she needed Aldebarian friends.

"The council is holding an inquiry. I'm afraid an armed Narr escort is on the way to take you to their chamber." Shual had a note of gravity in his voice.

"What can I tell them I haven't reported already?" Kelli's frustration bubbled out. "If they think I'm responsible, why don't they just say so?"

"That is not their way. For now, they are looking for technology, so they want to know about how you could save the Earth shuttle carrying your team. The Narr have stirred up powerful feelings against Lord Ravon, and against your team."

"Only a fool would believe those lies," Duncan fumed. "Without Kelli, we would all be dead."

"You are correct, Dr. Meddars. But there are some who are not interested in hearing the truth." Shual's voice became soothing. "This one is here to help. We will go to the council ahead of the escort. There you will find some friends, some enemies. They will want to examine your technology."

"I'm not turning over Eric to them." Kelli's voice remained soft and even, but her eyes showed the fury inside.

"Would you consider turning it over to the Degg? It will be under the protection of the high lord of Deggar. This one, who is your friend, would have access to the program, and would be present when we examine it."

Kelli looked from Shual to Michael. Michael Gentry's quick nod signaled his agreement. "Yes, of course. What do I tell the council?"

"Speak as little as possible, but always the truth. The high lord of Deggar will guide you, and whenever possible let him speak for you. This is the way of our people." Shual seemed relieved that Kelli had agreed. "We must go now. Rom Nashi will delay the escort long enough for us to arrive ahead of them."

They arrived ahead of the escort. Guards ushered them before the council members.

"How did you get here? Where is the escort?" spat Lord Gorron, rising from his seat in fury. He was the most monstrous creature Kelli could imagine; all bloated cranium perched on a twisted frame. His eyes shone like dark pits of evil. His voice spewed hate.

"The Earth people are our guests. Since the council is meeting in the Deggar homeland, I invited them to join us. A guest needs an invitation, not an armed escort." The high lord of Deggar's words were gracious and appreciated.

"They're spies and murderers. Were not your own people's children killed on their shuttle?" Gorron's voiced mellowed to an oily hiss. "Do their lives mean nothing to you?"

"All Degg cherish their young, it is our way. But we would not dishonor their memory by accusing these people of their murder without proof." The high lord's voice remained calm. "They have come here to answer our questions of their own accord. Let us not waste their time with bickering."

Lord Travalla, last surviving member of the Royal family of Shamar and head of the Council of Unity, swiveled his chair around and looked down on the lesser members of the council from his place on the platform. "I agree. Proceed with questioning, but do not forget they are guests."

"We demand you turn the spy technology over to us. We will examine it, and thereby prove that these 'guests' are guilty of murder." Careful planning and well-placed rumors gave Lord Gorron confidence and arrogance, and though his mind contained the knowledge of a million ancestors, he forgot that most basic of principles. Never underestimate your enemy.

"Lord Gorron is wise. We have asked Miss Royal to turn over the device and are happy to report that she has done so. Our communications expert, Senior Programmer Shual, will examine it, unless Lord Gorron has someone more capable in mind." The humility in the voice and manner would have commanded an Oscar on Earth. Kelli, standing beside Shual with her eyes lowered, choked off a chuckle. This was a high stakes game, and unless she was mistaken, the high lord of Deggar had called Lord Gorron's bluff.

"Who told you to interfere in this matter, Degg?

Everyone here knows of your alliance with Lord Ravon," Lord Gorron bellowed, as if he could change the fact that they had outmaneuvered him with the sheer volume of his voice.

"Does Lord Gorron doubt Shual will give an honest and accurate report?" Now the Deggarian lord's voice grew pained. That someone would cast doubt upon the integrity of a Degg, on the honor of all Degg, was a serious insult. A master gamesman, he had the Narr lord in check.

"See that you report promptly, and don't think you have fooled this council. You forget that not everyone plays your games," snarled Gorron.

"You forget who heads this council." Lord Travalla pounded a fist on the table and then pointed at Lord Gorron. "While I am that head, you will conduct yourself with more decorum. This council has not given you the authority to demand anything."

Checkmate, Kelli thought as she raised her eyes, expecting to see at least a hint of smugness on the Degg's face. There was none. Perhaps it was beneath the dignity of a Degg to gloat, but it wasn't beneath hers. She gave Gorron her most pitying look, preparing some scathing remark, something worthy of the contempt he deserved. Before she could deliver it, Duncan's voice was whispering in her ear, soothing her ruffled feelings and advising caution. They had won this round without her even speaking one word. They could celebrate later at the open school.

***

Lord Travalla prepared to dismiss the council and assembly. He would have a private word later with the high lord of Deggar, and with Lord Ravon. They were up to something, something besides baiting Gorron's temper, and he had best know what it was. Lord Ravon was in enough difficulties these days without provoking the Narr leader.

Travalla's own secretary, hurrying into the chamber to announce the high priestess of Nellar and a full delegation of

Nellari with her, interrupted his thoughts. Lord Travalla stood to welcome the priestess. Everyone on the council stood to honor Galandra, whose rare visits outside Nellar always preceded some momentous news or event.

"My greetings, Lord Travalla." Galandra returned his bow, long hair falling forward over her face. It was a beautiful face for one of her age, but not uncommon for Nellari. "How is my sister, your wife?"

"She is most happy. What brings the Nellari high priestess so far from home?" Lord Travalla answered. Nellari were keepers of the land, the animals, and the magic of Aldebar. Galandra was their greatest seer.

"Curiosity. It isn't every day we have visitors from another world. Are these the humans?" The high priestess walked toward the small group without waiting for an answer.

***

Kelli admired Galandra's erect posture and graceful, fluid movements. A ballerina moved like that, making you think she was floating on air. When she came closer, Kelli could see the intricate tattoos on her arms, her face, and on her small bare feet.

Shual, who seemed awestruck in Galandra's presence, made the one-sided introductions. "This is Dr. Michael Gentry, leader of the humans at Rishal."

Galandra placed her hand flat against Michael's chest, her eyes focused above his head. "An honorable man. Dr. Gentry, you serve your people well."

"This is Dr. Duncan Meddars, a professor on the team." Shual's voice shook as if he were seeking the right tone to convey the proper respect.

When Galandra laid her hand against Duncan's chest, she smiled and looked him in the eyes. "A human seer, and a powerful one. I did not expect such a pleasure."

"The pleasure is mine, and the honor," Duncan replied, emulating Shual's bow.

"This is Kelli Royal. She is a student from Earth," Shual continued, motioning Kelli toward the high priestess.

Galandra placed her hand on Kelli's head, then stepped back and studied her face. Reaching out, she pulled Kelli toward her and whispered in her ear, "Welcome home."

She did not speak the words loud enough for anyone else to hear, but Kelli heard. It was the voice from her dream. She stood there frozen for a moment, not knowing what to say. Then Galandra turned and walked toward the council members before she could say anything.

Galandra addressed Lord Travalla again, this time in his official position instead of as her brother-in-law. "Are the Nellari represented on this council?"

"We represent all peoples here. The Nellari seats are vacant by their choice, and have been for as long as this council has stood," Lord Travalla answered, looking at Galandra with a puzzled expression. "With no disrespect, my lady, Nellari are known to be uninterested in politics, choosing to vote on rare occasions via a Deggarian proxy."

"I wish then to present the Nellari delegation. I hope they will fill their duties to the council as expected." The news brought a wave of silence, followed by the hum of quick excited discussion among small groups of council members as they digested it. Surprise caught even the Nellari's closest allies, though unlike Lord Gorron, they were pleased by the unexpected turn of events.

"Witch. What right have you to be here? You hold no political office in Nellar or on this council," spat Gorron.

"Fear makes you whine, Lord Gorron. Silence at least would hide your cowardice. This delegation is quite official, as am I as their leader." Galandra waved several Nellari into the chamber. She handed official papers to Lord Travalla, and he called for a vote of confirmation. They admitted the Nellari as members of the council in good standing.

The humans, their presence overshadowed by the dramatic

entrance of the Nellari delegation, watched in silence for over an hour before Lord Travalla thanked them and said they could leave.

Kelli walked behind Duncan, Galandra's words echoing in her mind.

"Professor Gentry." Galandra reached out her hand. "Not everyone on our world listens to rumors. Please bring your students for a visit to Nellar — they will be welcome."

"Thank you, Priestess, your offer is most gracious." Michael's tone was light. "That is what we have come for. We are here to meet and get to know the peoples of Aldebar, and to see their lands."

Walking out, Kelli considered Galandra's words. Perhaps the translator had made a mistake. Maybe Galandra had meant to welcome Kelli to her home world and nothing more. Michael and Duncan walked ahead, talking together about the council visit. Shual walked by her side without speaking. She ventured a question. "What do you think of Galandra? Shual? Shual?"

"Oh, my apologies, Miss Royal. This one believes you wish to know if the high priestess is an ally. She is a powerful lady, a seer of course, but also a wise leader." Shual appeared ruffled by the day's events.

"What do you think of her invitation? Should we go?" Kelli's questions were perceptive, and the silence that followed them was disturbing. "Shual?"

"Yes, of course you will go. It is not an invitation one would decline. The Nellari are friends to the Degg. The high lord of Deggar will make the arrangements." Shual was speaking to her, but his mind seemed far away.

"But?" Kelli pressed for more, wanted to know what he had not said.

"The Nellari are particular about who they allow into their homeland. There must be a reason for the invitation." Shual answered as if speaking a riddle aloud.

"But Galandra is on our side, isn't she?" Kelli asked.

"She is no friend of the Narr," Shual answered.

***

A few days later, the Aldebarian students were abuzz with news that the Narr had reached Rishal. After meeting Lord Gorron, it did not surprise Kelli to overhear many students express fear and anger at their arrival.

She made her way to the cafeteria with Ammie and Marla, but halted when she noticed the new students seated at a table. She stared at the newcomers — these must be Narr. They looked nothing like the Narr lord she had seen at the meeting. They were pale-skinned, and might have passed as humans except for their star-shaped irises. One student noticed her look and met her gaze with an arrogant, hostile look.

An audible sniff caught her attention, and she noticed one of the Narr students sitting at a table alone with her head down. She appeared to be crying. A Narr pointed at the girl and laughed. "Poor little drudge is crying."

Kelli went through the line and filled her tray. She walked past the table where Ammie and Marla were talking to two handsome Bengari students. They had saved her a seat, but she sat down next to the Narr girl, who was still crying to the apparent delight of her fellow students.

"Are you okay?" she asked as she sweetened her tea.

"You should not sit here. I am a dishonored child of traitors," the girl mumbled.

Ignoring the comment, Kelli introduced herself. "My name is Kelli. I come from Earth."

Giving a soft gasp, the girl grabbed up her tray and hurried from the room.

The table of Narr students roared with laughter.

Kelli was about to deliver a stinging rebuke when a gentle hand touched her shoulder. She looked around to find Shual standing there.

"Hold your tongue, friend; your anger will not help the girl." Shual took a seat beside her.

Kelli lowered her voice and asked, "Why are they so mean to her?"

Shual nodded, "Rom Nashi informed us of Nalta. Lord Gorron accused her parents of treason and had them executed. They have sentenced her to life as a lowly drudge. To dispel any disharmony in their homeland, they have sent her here to await her assimilation."

"That is so unfair. She isn't responsible for her parents' actions," Kelli said.

Shual reached over and took her hand. "You cannot save everyone. To try will make things worse for her and create conflict with the Narr."

Kelli nodded her understanding, but determined to befriend the girl and make her life easier while she was at the school.

"I have good news," Shual said. "We have made the arrangements for your visit to Nellar."

"So soon?" Kelli grinned with excitement, and thoughts of the Narr girl flittered to the back of her mind.

CHAPTER TWENTY-ONE
—ALDEBAR PRIME—NELLARI HOMELAND

A week later, Kelli sat with the other students onboard a transport shuttle as it landed in the Nellari homeland. As the door opened, a rush of warm humid air filled the transport, heavy with the smells of exotic flowers, animals, and rich soil. Kelli breathed in, tasting the heavy sweet atmosphere, so different from the dry clean air of Rishal. Duncan and several of the students began reacting to the foreign pollen by sneezing.

At first glance, the capital of the Nellari homeland appeared to be a tropical jungle. Kelli could see colorful trees, magnificent flowers, and unusual plants everywhere. The students snapped holographic pictures even before they stepped down from the transport.

Outside, she could see the landing pad, and in the distance what appeared to be a city. A Nellari delegation welcomed them. The official was a Nellari male covered in elaborate tattoos. He introduced himself as Orron, and then began his duties as their guide. He said, "The city itself is about two miles away. We will walk from here, please take off your shoes."

As they removed socks and shoes, the students joked among themselves. The Nellari did not believe in shoes. The trail, for it was too narrow for a road, was a mixture of soft earth, straw, and dry leaves. It felt soft and warm to Kelli's feet as she walked.

The plants looked familiar, yet exotic. Sounds came from the undergrowth as some small animal scurried from their approach. Kelli looked but couldn't see what it was.

By Earth standards, the Nellari capital was a primitive city. There were no skyscrapers, no high-rise buildings of any kind. Kelli was struck by the magnificence of their architecture. The Nellari had carved each building from blocks of fine white marble. Kelli studied the patterns etched in the stone and highlighted with gold, silver, or black. They passed stalls along the main road, selling a wide variety of fruits and vegetables, and trinkets of all kinds.

The Earth students soon became the center of attention for a group of young Nellari. They offered samples of a fruit called pylon. It was sweet and refreshing, but the juice left everyone's mouth stained blue.

"You're afraid to try new things," Kelli teased Duncan. "It's delicious."

"It's blue, and so are your lips." Duncan laughed as he handed her his handkerchief. Much of the stain came off, but it would need water and soap to remove all of it.

High Priestess Galandra was hosting a special banquet in their honor, and Kelli hoped to freshen up before it began. The heat from the walk and the bright sun made her wish she was wearing one of the gauzy dresses that the Nellari women wore. A striking purple garment caught her eye, and she succumbed to the urge to buy it. The Nellari merchant showed Kelli how to attach the gown to a silver neckband, and then added a matching silver belt. The effect seemed to please the merchant, so Kelli bought these too.

After letting the students shop and explore for a few hours, Orron announced that it was time to get ready for the banquet. He guided them to a bathhouse. Kelli soaked in the fragrant water, then rubbed the soft leaves across her body. The leaves served a dual purpose; to dry the body, and to apply soothing oils to the skin. Feeling clean and refreshed, she dressed in the new garment and twisted up her damp hair. A soft whistle and smile from Duncan rewarded her efforts and gave her confidence.

The banquet was much more casual than anything they had been to in Rishal, where the high meal was always formal. Scattered tables laden with exotic foods were spaced throughout the large room. Guests and hosts helped themselves as they mingled. The fruits and vegetables were larger, fresher, and tasted sweeter than in Rishal. When Kelli commented on this, Shual explained that the Nellari homeland produced seventy percent of the Aldebar's produce, and it was superior to anything grown in the other homelands.

"Are you enjoying your stay on Aldebar?"

The question caused Kelli to turn to see who was speaking to her. Galandra was standing behind her, holding a glass of wine. Something in her tone said the question had a dual meaning. After their first encounter, Kelli knew Galandra had answers to the mysteries of her heritage.

"Yes, now that that horrible mess about the shuttle explosion is over," Kelly answered.

"I imagine it was hard to leave your family. You must get homesick." Galandra's voice was soothing, her eyes sharp and probing.

"My father died in a shuttle accident when I was young, and my mother died of cancer three years ago. The students are my family now." Kelli used part of the truth to avoid betraying her mission, but Galandra continued to probe.

"Were you close to your father?" Galandra began leading them to a more private area of the room. "It must have been hard to lose him at such a young age."

"Yes, we were very close. I took his death very hard."

Kelli didn't say that she had adored her father, and

that she still wasn't over the effects of his disappearance, but Galandra seemed to pull the feelings from her. There was a look on Galandra's face of genuine compassion, as if she shared Kelli's pain. That, of course, had to be Kelli's imagination. She sipped the glass of sweet wine that someone handed her, feeling a relaxing sensation spreading throughout her body. The thought that Galandra might try to read her thoughts flittered through the haze clouding her mind, but she didn't care. This peaceful sensation was too strong.

"Look at me." Galandra's soft voice was a command. The eyes that met Kelli's still held compassion, but they were probing with a purpose. After a few minutes, Galandra's face contorted with pain and she pulled back with tears in her eyes, whispering, "Poor child."

***

Duncan found Kelli standing alone sipping wine, a vacant smile on her face. He asked, "Are you okay?"

"What? Oh yes. In fact, I feel wonderful." Studying her glass for a moment, she added, "This wine is wonderful. We should take a bottle back to Rishal."

A frown furrowed Duncan's brow. He took the glass from Kelli and smelled its contents. There was something strange going on. Kelli appeared drugged, and he feared Galandra's involvement. He scanned the room until he saw Michael talking with Shual. He motioned for them to come. They responded to his worried expression and hurried over.

"Is there a problem, Dr. Meddars?" Shual asked as he came up. Then he noticed the way Kelli was standing and humming to herself. He looked at the glass. "May I?"

"What's going on?" Michael asked, his voice loud. Several Nellari turned to see what was wrong.

"One moment please, Dr. Gentry." Shual put one finger into the wine and tasted it. "Of all the bad manners. Someone has added a tranquilizer to this drink; it lowers one's resistance to a mind probe. Who was talking to her? We will report this to—"

"Galandra," Duncan broke in, indignation rising inside him.

"Yes, we will report it to Galandra, but who was last talking to Miss Royal?" Shual repeated.

"I told you. She was talking to Galandra," Duncan answered.

"Oh my, this is most unusual. One is of an opinion that we should leave now." Shual seemed at a loss for what to tell them. Using drugs on someone without their consent was against Nellari law, but who could they report Galandra to? The high priestess was the center of the Nellari government, her word law.

"Not until I have a word with Galandra," Michael said, He was furious. All this hospitality had been nothing more than a guise to lure Kelli here.

Orron made his way to their group. He greeted them and then addressed Duncan. "Dr. Meddars, Galandra wishes to speak to you...alone. Please follow me."

The summons startled Duncan, but he nodded agreement and turned to Michael. "Stay here with Kelli, and if I'm not back in thirty minutes, get everyone together and leave."

"Perhaps I should accompany you," Shual began.

Orron insisted that the high priestess wished to speak to the human seer alone.

"Let's go," Duncan snapped.

Following Orron from the banquet hall, he willed himself to remain calm. Losing his temper would not help the situation. They soon arrived at a door where Orron activated the open sequence. Galandra waited inside.

"Thank you for coming, Dr. Meddars," Galandra began, and then she turned to Orron. "You may go now."

"Someone drugged one of my students, and I believe you had something to do with it," Duncan said when the doors closed behind Orron.

"You're very direct, Dr. Meddars, and angry. I assure you that the sedative is quite harmless. My grandniece will recover from its effects soon." Galandra studied his shocked face. "You knew why she came here, didn't you?"

"Yes, of course, I...." Duncan felt as if someone had literally knocked the breath out of him. It took a moment to regain his composure, and when he did, the anger dissipated. "Did you say niece?"

"Yes, though to be accurate, I am a grandaunt, as you would reckon ancestry," Galandra answered. She poured Duncan a glass of wine and then laughed at his look of concern. "No, it's not drugged."

Embarrassed that she had read his thoughts, Duncan took the glass and swallowed the sweet drink. If what Galandra said was true, why was she telling him instead of Kelli? Why had she used drugs to read Kelli's mind? There was one way to find out, so he asked. "If you know who she is, why didn't you say something? Why use drugs and mind probes?"

"I needed to know if she suspected the truth about her heritage, and what her feelings toward her father are. I asked to speak to you because you're her friend. She trusts you, and sad news comes easier from a friend." Galandra paused, watching to see if Duncan understood. Her meaning struck him like a hammer. She went on. "Her father died when he returned to Aldebar eight years ago."

"You want me to break the news to her. It won't be easy; she's been looking for him for many years." Duncan knew Galandra's suggestion made sense, but he hated to be the one to do it, to see Kelli's eyes filled with sadness and loss.

"Give her some good news as well. She has grandparents and other family members here on Aldebar. They will want to meet her." Galandra's voice was soothing. "For now, I ask that you keep this as quiet as possible. I've waited a long time for Holba's daughter to come home, but there are others who will not welcome her."

"Are you telling me that Kelli would be in some kind of danger if it becomes known that she is your niece?" Duncan's question was blunt.

"You are quick to catch onto the obvious. Keep a watchful eye on her." Galandra nodded toward the door to signal that the meeting was over. "Thank you for coming, Dr. Meddars. I have much to think on that may require your services later."

When she did not elaborate, Duncan joined Kelli and Michael in the banquet hall. He could read the questions in their eyes, but felt it best not to discuss his meeting with Galandra until they returned to Rishal. Kelli, who was still recovering from the drug, slept on the return trip.

Back at the open school, Duncan broke the news as gently as he could, watching Kelli's reaction. She was hard to read, keeping her emotions bottled up inside, sometimes allowing them to escape, but seldom sharing them. There were no tears, but he could tell she was about to cry as she asked questions.

***

"Did she say how he died? Who he was? There's so much I still don't know." Kelli's voice sounded as if she were fighting for the energy to speak. After all this time, after coming halfway across the universe, it had all been for nothing. Her father had died soon after he disappeared. There would be no reunion, happy or otherwise. They might never answer her questions.

"You can ask your grandparents those questions. Galandra seemed sure they would be eager to meet you." It was the first time he had mentioned her grandparents, and he tried to sound encouraging.

"Grandparents? Galandra told you I have grandparents?" A flicker of hope and joy lit her eyes. This was something Kelli hadn't even considered. The sooner she met them, the better. It disappointed her that Galandra hadn't said who or where they were. They would contact her, and she must wait. Most bizarre of all was the revelation that Galandra was her father's aunt. It puzzled her to learn that she was in danger and needed security. "I've evaded enough security, or outsmarted it, to know that the best security often fails."

Duncan provided a bastion of support. Sneaking out to a secluded area known as the Meditation Garden, he held her as she allowed herself to cry. Kelli absorbed his warmth, his strength as they sat talking in soft whispers.

"You always seem to be around when I fall apart. I'm sorry."

He made no secret of his growing feelings, without pushing or pressuring. He had plans, dreams that included her, but this wasn't the time to share those.

They talked of more mundane things and admired the surroundings. The "garden" had no, or little, plant life. What it had were beautiful rock formations of every imaginable size, shape, and color. Several were translucent crystals, their colors reflected on the walkway leading up to the bench where they sat.

"What if they don't want to see me?" It was impossible for Kelli's mind to escape long.

"Who wouldn't want to see you? You're beautiful." Duncan's voice was light, teasing. "I want to see you all the time."

That remark brought a smile. Kelli knew she would wait for her grandparents to contact her. But if they didn't, or if things went wrong, she had people who loved her, a place where she belonged. It was late when they left the garden and went to their separate rooms.

***

The next morning Kelli took a breakfast tray and headed toward the table where the Narr girl, Nalta, sat. The girl looked up and smiled. It had taken time to win her over, but now she seemed to welcome Kelli's companionship.

"Are students on Earth free to choose their life paths? Can they be whatever they want?" she asked.

Kelli nodded with a smile; someone had been studying Earth culture. According to Nalta, the Narr lords decided everyone's future. In fact, it was common to them to punish the young for the transgressions of even ancient ancestors.

"I'm going to run away," Nalta whispered.

"Are you sure? What will happen if they catch you?"

"They will kill me, but that's better than having my memories stolen and being made a drudge."

"Please be careful," Kelli whispered back. "Maybe I can help."

After the meal, Kelli went straight to Shual for advice. He shook his head with dismay. "They will indeed kill the girl. It is their law. You were wise to trust this one with the knowledge."

"Can you help?" Kelli asked.

"One can try, but you must distance yourself. Do not mention this to anyone. Nalta has put you in danger by sharing her plans."

"But she is my friend," Kelli said.

"As are you mine. Trust that, and we will see what we can do for the girl. One hears rumors."

"Rumors?"

"That's enough for now. It is better that you do not know everything."

CHAPTER TWENTY-TWO

Shual entered his apartment early, He instructed his special assistant Cort to contact him in case of emergency, and sent a message on the most secure of lines to Rom Nebbar inquiring about the Narr assimilation process, and what happened if someone refused it. The inquiry couched in the broadest terms mentioned nothing about a specific Narr student, or Kelli's involvement. After he sent his message, Shual questioned his wisdom in offering to help. He pushed back from his terminal. This message was not the reason for his return home.

He understood how important it was for him to examine the Earth cognizant program. It had taken several days to make sure he could launch "Eric" without endangering others. He would, of course, report the findings to his lord, but other members of the council could wait.

Shual opened his computer. There was no way Eric could access any networks. As soon as he had turned the power on, the small holographic Eric appeared above the screen.

"Identify yourself. Where is Kelli? Why am I being confined? There is no room to activate any of my functions," the faint voice asked. The image flickered, and Shual wondered if he needed to increase Eric's function to communicate.

"This one is sure we met once during the trip to Aldebar.

We are endeavoring to protect Kelli. She is well, and wishes you to be in my custody for the time being."

"You must release me. Kelli is in danger."

Shual shook his head. "She is in no imminent danger. We must deactivate the part of your programing that acts as her protection before we can reunite you with her."

"Impossible, you cannot delete one of my primary functions."

Shual turned his head from side to side. Kelli said the program's image was that of its designer, Eric Fendler. Designing a program in one's own image spoke of a vanity that was almost beyond comprehension. Still, perhaps he could reason with Eric. Kelli had spoken of her friend with fondness. He had saved her life. That was a bond they shared.

"You are putting the entire exchange in danger." Shual spoke as if to a child.

"I must have more room. I am functioning at 18%. It is not enough," the program insisted.

Shual's mouth rippled as he let out an audible sigh. "We seem to be at an impasse. I cannot give you more power without putting us all in danger." He shut the program down, noting the flicker of surprise on the face of the hologram as it disappeared.

Looking around, he wondered how he could further insulate the room. He began studying the data he had recorded about the remarkable program. The potential for increased power fascinated him. How much further could he increase its power and range? What were its limits?

***

An imperious buzzing came from the outer door of Shual's chambers. It was far too insistent to be a Degg. Shual closed the door to his computer room, securing Eric behind a barrier of metal and electronic shields. It had been their second talk, and they were still at an impasse.

The door slid open, and he stepped back, just managing

not to collapse to the floor in surprise. There at the very door of his quarters stood the high lord of Deggar himself, a figure worthy of reverence. A Nellari official and the Bengari captain from the Earth voyage accompanied him. Shual was certain the Bengari's hand had been on the buzzer.

Meditation candles and his new tranquility stone lay near his couch. Shual blinked in shame. Such disorder was inexcusable.

"My most honorable lord," Shual stammered, and then stepped aside so they could enter.

The high lord bowed in return. He inclined a hand toward the Nellari. "This is Bannis. Galandra assigned him to represent her in all matters here in Deggar." He motioned to the Bengari and said, "I believe you remember Captain Raggion from your time aboard his vessel."

Shual swallowed and answered, "Yes, my lord."

"You made inquiries about Narr dissidents," Raggion interjected.

The high lord sighed, and Bannis rolled his eyes in disapproval of Raggion's impatience.

Shual hung his head, wondering how much trouble he was about to get into for his latest attempt to aid Kelli. "A most innocuous inquiry, my lord."

"Perhaps I can help you," Bannis said. "Are you in fact concerned for a Narr female, Nalta, who is a student at the open school here in Rishal? Their records show they scheduled her for involuntary assimilation."

Shual met Bannis's eyes. His voice squeaked, "Yes, my lord."

Bannis smiled. "Good. Galandra wishes you to aid me in freeing the girl."

Shual's mouth formed its largest possible circle, with lips stretched waveless and tight, but no sound came out. He reached for a chair, anything to steady himself.

"My personal aid, Shual, is most honored to be of any

service to Lady Galandra," said the high lord.

Personal assistant? Shual crumbled to the floor. Captain Raggion put his hands under Shual's arms and hauled him to his feet. Shual straightened and said weakly, "How may I assist you?"

Bannis bowed and explained, "Many years ago the Nellari, along with others, created a sanctuary for dissidents from the Narr Homeland. It is one of the most guarded secrets on Aldebar. Neither Captain Raggion nor I can visit the open school without creating a great deal of suspicion. You are there often to meet with the Earth exchange students. You could get a message to the Narr student, and help her rendezvous with Bannis and Captain Raggion."

Shual put forth a weak argument. "Why would she trust me or my message?"

That brought a bark of laughter from Raggion, and he struck Shual on the back. "Not trust a Degg? Impossible. Everyone knows how honorable the Degg are."

Shual listened to the details of what seemed a simple enough plan. In three days, he would slip her a message and then wait for her outside the school. He would transport her across the city and deliver her to Captain Raggion and Bannis. They would take her to sanctuary. It sounded so simple.

After his guests had gone, Shual lit every candle. He retrieved his new mediation stone but threw it on his couch. What kind of Nellari web had he gotten into? Who had cursed him? What had brought him to the attention of so many important people? The high lord of Deggar, the priestess of Nellar, heir of the Shamaru leader, a wealthy Bengari captain, and a powerful Narr lord now knew him by name. He covered his head and shook in fear. After Shual composed himself, he contacted his personal assistant Cort to inform him of their rise in status and upcoming move to the capital.

***

It was several days before Shual had time to access the advanced Earth program. He improved the electronic shielding so he could increase the power of Eric without risking possible infiltration of the Aldebarian network.

The hologram was larger and much more distinct. "What do you want now?" The voice sounded petulant.

"What this one has always desired. I need your help," Shual replied. "I have restored your power as requested."

The hologram bowed. "You have questions?"

"Let's start with something basic. Why would such an advanced program choose this simple holographic means to communicate?"

Eric snorted, which Shual found offensive. It had been a legitimate question.

"My dear Deggarian programmer, I would have expected you to figure that one out. The human brain could not handle the direct input. That would damage the limited brain matter. This form allows the eyes and ears to serve as their normal receptors. Kelli's neural disk allows us to locate and communicate over distances."

"Of course," Shual said, nodding in understanding. He reached to a small pouch beside him. Inside were two small disks containing millions of bits of information. One was everything he could find on the Narr dissidents, and the other contained information on the peoples of Aldebar.

"Why should I be interested in helping you?" the hologram asked. His eyes narrowed, and Shual got a sense of its creator and namesake.

Shual raised a finger toward his lips. "You should rather ask how I could help you. Your designer created you to function at what he termed L-7. Modesty restrains me to say only that this one is a more gifted programmer. It is probable that we can increase your function to L-10 in a short amount of time."

"And what do you want from me?"

Shual tapped his fingers in front of the disks. "I need your help in discovering who murdered Kelli's father, and in protecting her."

"A common goal, one that we will accomplish."

Shual loaded the data and could almost feel the program sigh with pleasure.

"More...," came the voice.

"Enough for today," Shual said before shutting down.

***

Shual slipped a message to Nalta. The message instructed her to meet him in three nights and not to tell anyone, not even Kelli. It was important to keep the Earth students out of this. She nodded without turning to look at him. He watched from the front of the cafeteria until the ink dissolved. She surprised him by rolling the note into a ball and putting it in her cup before Kelli joined her at the table.

Shual talked with Michael Gentry for a few minutes and then left the cafeteria. That evening he met with Eric. He was thinking of the program as a person. He even taught Eric a few Deggarian games of logic. That night Eric won.

"I distract you, brother Shual," Eric said, effecting the tone and manners of a Degg.

"This one will help the Narr girl to escape, and then they will take her to a place known as Sanctuary. One has considered this, and cannot come up with any location on Aldebar that would be safe for Narr dissidents."

"Perhaps it is not on Aldebar."

"Where else could it be?"

"Something orbiting the planet, a base or a small moon. A Bengari vessel could reach that in a short time."

"Impossible. Who could make any of our known moons habitable?"

"Your data is full of information about the Nellari. Would it be within their power to develop terraforming?"

Shual thought of the rich Nellari homeland created from much the same deserts his people inhabited that provided much of the planet's food. "It is not impossible,"

"And wasn't Captain Raggion among the conspirators who planned the girl's escape?"

Shual nodded. "You have given this one much to think on."

"I could give you much more if you freed me," the program pleaded.

"As yet, that is not safe," Shual answered, and shut the program down before his hesitation revealed too much uncertainty. He had already increased the program to Level-10.

CHAPTER TWENTY-THREE
—ALDEBAR PRIME—SHAMARU HOMELAND

Lord Travalla's conference room was large enough to hold a dozen or more, but it was empty now except for Lord Travalla and Lord Ravon. Lord Travalla had announced that one visitor from Earth was his granddaughter, the heir to the Travalla family. Most of the homeland was in a state of shock, uncertain what this news would mean to their people. Lord Ravon stood frozen in place by the announcement. This granddaughter he spoke of was the earth girl who caused such turmoil in Rishal.

"So speak, Ravon, tell me what you're thinking," Lord Travalla began.

"I am at a loss, my lord. I did not know that such a thing was even possible." Lord Ravon avoided asking why Travalla had kept him in the dark about such an important announcement. Everyone assumed he would one day take over Travalla's seat as ruler of Shamar. Perhaps Travalla was rethinking that decision. He continued. "I am surprised that you recognized this Earth woman as your granddaughter. I doubt she will take your place on the council. There wouldn't be enough support in the homeland."

"You will follow me on the council. I have also signed a proclamation that no alien born person can represent Shamaru on the Council of Unity." Travalla phrased the next statement with care. "I have other plans for my granddaughter. She will ensure that my family's line carries on and rules Shamar as it has for thousands of years."

"But you said that no human can rule in Shamar." Lord Ravon tensed. Perhaps Travalla intended to separate the powers of the council from those of the homeland.

"Her son could rule, if he were born in Shamar, if he were also your son." Travalla's voice and his eyes seemed to see this far-off event.

"What are you suggesting?" Ravon demanded. If Lord Travalla had lost his reasoning, there was more trouble than he realized.

"What do you remember of my son, Holba Shar?" Travalla asked, waiting for Ravon to answer.

"Not a lot. I was a young man when he left on the Earth mission, and he died soon after he came back," Ravon answered, watching Travalla.

"I had arranged for him to marry your mother. Do you remember that? It was a perfect alliance of families, but they didn't love each other," Lord Travalla continued. "Your marriage to my granddaughter would fulfill that agreement between our families."

"And what makes you think she will go along with this? Humans are independent people. She may refuse or be married to someone else." Ravon could see Travalla's plan now. With an alliance between the two most powerful families in Shamar, Travalla's control of the homeland would be stronger than ever. This would guarantee Ravon had little opposition when Travalla nominated him. It was brilliant.

"My granddaughter came all this way to find her heritage. We will give her a destiny." Travalla's enthusiasm for his own plan grew as he verbalized it. "Everyone is susceptible to flattery; woo her, win her heart, and convince her to marry you."

"You make it sound easy. Have you met this woman? I have, and I doubt she succumbs to flattery." Ravon remembered his encounters with the Earth woman. She was beautiful enough, but what kind of wife she might make was less certain.

"I have Galandra's word that she is an honorable woman, and has a great respect for her father's memory. Also, I've been told that her treatment on Earth has not always been kind. She may not be eager to return there. I could tell you more, but some things are better kept private," Lord Travalla said. Looking at Ravon, he added. "I have invited her to visit Shamar soon. Can you be here?"

"Of course. The sooner we begin, the sooner there can be a wedding." Ravon knew there had been no doubt in Lord Travalla's mind that he would accept. They both understood their duty to the homeland.

CHAPTER TWENTY-FOUR
—Aldebar Prime—Degg Homeland

It took two weeks for the invitation to arrive, two agonizing weeks of waiting, and hoping, and fearing that her grandparents didn't want to meet her. Shual delivered the handwritten letter from her grandmother, Lady Nellandra, wife of the ranking lord of Shamar, Lord Travalla. Kelli sat frozen in shock. Never in her wildest imaginings had she imagined the son of such a powerful political figure as her father. Her hands shook as she opened the letter and read.

The letter was everything Kelli had hoped for. It began with the greeting "Dear Child," and expressed Nellandra's joy at having a granddaughter and her eagerness to meet her and to hear about her son's life on Earth. Tentative arrangements were being made for Kelli to visit Shamar during an upcoming break from school, subject to Kelli's approval. The purposed visit would last for three weeks, during which the Earth team would stay in the home of Lord Travalla and tour the Shamaru homeland.

"Shall I send an acceptance letter?" Shual's voice penetrated the avalanche of thoughts crashing through her mind. Kelli looked up, and when their eyes met, she realized Shual had known all along the identity of her grandparents and had withheld that information for weeks.

"Of course, I'll accept." Kelli stammered. "Why didn't you tell me?"

"If Lord Travalla had chosen not to acknowledge the relationship, it would have been awkward for me to reveal his name," Shual answered. "As a ranking member of the Council of Unity, we afford him a certain amount of privacy."

"Well, I hope I meet with his approval," Kelli snapped, and then regretted her words. "I'm sorry, Shual, that was unfair. The letter is so kind, and it must have been a surprise for them to find out about me."

"It has caused quite a stir," Shual agreed. "Lady Nellandra has been the center of controversy for years. She hopes to spare you some of her experiences."

"I wasn't expecting anything like this, but I'm ready to find out about my father's family." Kelli brushed back her hair. "Does Professor Gentry know yet?"

"I thought it best that you be the one to discuss this matter with him."

"Thank you, I think you're right." Kelli wondered what Michael would think of this. She knew it would complicate the Aldebar Project, when things were settling down to a nice routine.

She found Duncan first and showed him the letter. He laughed and teased her about being a long-lost heiress.

The news surprised Michael, but did not seem to upset him. "We will all visit Shamar, an opportunity that would not have been ours if you had not discovered your father's family."

***

The next morning, a knock on her door awakened Kelli. Grabbing a robe, she hurried to answer it.

Rom Nashi, Michael, Shual, and two of the Narr students were standing in the hall. There wasn't room for everyone to crowd into her room.

"We can use the meeting room at the end of the hall," Rom Nashi said, and led the way. "This shouldn't take long."

"She knows something," one of the Narr students said. "She is always sitting with Nalta, even though everyone knows Nalta is a traitor's git."

Rom Nashi raised his hand and spoke in what was a very harsh tone for a Degg. "Silence. This is a serious matter, and we will only discuss it in private. If you cannot respect that, you will go to your room until we finish."

Kelli looked at the other faces. Michael looked puzzled and concerned. Shual appeared calm. He seemed almost pleased with himself, so she relaxed.

When they were all in the conference room and the door closed, Rom Nashi began.

"When is the last time you saw the Narr student, Nalta?"

"Last night at the high meal. Is something wrong?" Kelli replied with genuine concern in her voice.

"I'm afraid Nalta has disappeared. These students think she has run away, and that you have helped her."

Kelli shook her head. "No, I had nothing to do with her disappearance."

"That's a lie. She was always sitting with Nalta and whispering. They must have planned something," the other Narr student interrupted.

Rom Nashi motioned for silence and then turned to Kelli.

He'll know if I'm lying, she thought. She took a breath and twisted the truth as much as she dared.

"Nalta is my friend. I sit with her at meals because these two and the others harass her every day. She is always sad and afraid of receiving the punishment for her parent's crime. If she had shared any plans for running away, I would have reported it." That was true, because she had gone straight to Shual.

Rom Nashi seemed satisfied that the matter, at least her part of it, was closed. He sent the Narr students back to their room with a stern warning against gossiping.

Kelli knew it was better that she didn't discuss it with

Shual either. He seemed a little smug, and she took that as a sign of Nalta's safety.

She moved closer to listen to Rom Nashi, who was talking with Michael as they walked back down the hall.

"One expects the Narr lords will lodge a complaint against the school if the girl does not return, but do not worry yourself. They sent her here knowing she was what you call, 'A flight risk.'"

Kelli had followed them past her room, but had to stop and hurry back to change out of her nightclothes and robe.

***

Time passed, and soon Kelli and the team were aboard transport to Shamar. She had hesitated to make the journey, uncertain that she should intrude herself into their established lives. After Duncan assured her that her feelings were natural, Kelli realized she was experiencing fear of finding the answers she had been seeking for so many years. As usual, he was right. Now, here she was heading for Shamar, laughing and joking with the other students.

Their guide, a young Shamaru woman with pale blue and white wings, stood up and addressed the group. "The crew will serve you a small snack. It is a square of cocomand and juice to wash it down. The taste is bland, a lot like dried grass. You must eat the entire square to receive its protection from altitude sickness."

The flight attendant passed out the cocomand, and Kelli found it smelled and tasted like a hay square that she had once fed horses as a treat. The other students followed her example and ate. They were eager to focus on the magnification screens on their transport, allowing them a spectacular view of the planet as they traveled above the surface. The sky above the clouds shone a crisp rose color.

"Oh, my God, we're going to crash," came Klaus's voice from the seat behind her. Indeed, it looked as if their transport was heading straight into the cliffs. At the last minute it turned, and missing the rocky cliff, rose higher into the mountain. There was nervous laughter among the students.

Their guide stood again. "The Shamaru homeland is high in the mountain ranges of the northern hemisphere of Aldebar, an area inaccessible to most Aldebarians other than the Shamaru. The mountains have high jagged peaks so close together it makes using conventional air transport hazardous, if not impossible, for untrained pilots. Inside the homeland, most Shamaru travel by using their natural wings to fly. We will provide you small jet packs, which will allow you a certain amount of mobility while in Shamar."

That brought a whoop of excitement from all the students except Klaus.

The transport plane landed in the outermost city of Shandar. The guide told them her ancestors had carved the city into the mountain, with its entrance built into the mouth of a giant cave. There were layers of the city up the mountain face and back inside the mountain itself. Winged Shamaru flew up and down between the levels of the city.

Ravon was there to greet them, a much more conciliatory Lord Ravon. He seemed to study Kelli as if seeing her for the first time.

Kelli nodded to him with a cool smile, assuming he was singling her out because of her newfound Shamaru family's status. It was hard to maintain her aloofness because, when he tried, Lord Ravon could be a charming and witty guide. He was definitely trying. If it had been anyone else, she would have said he was flirting with her. Duncan apparently thought so, because he stepped between them and placed an arm protectively around her shoulder.

That was a back off signal. Ravon scowled and moved away to talk to Michael and Peter about the architecture they were admiring.

"Lord Ravon has become quite a lady's man," Duncan remarked dryly.

"I'm sure he's trying to please Lord Travalla." Kelli couldn't bring herself to say grandfather, not before she was sure he accepted her.

"He had something else on his mind," Duncan continued. He had sensed that Lord Ravon had a purpose for his attention, and seen how Ravon had admired Kelli's tall, slender figure when she wasn't looking.

"I believe you're jealous, Dr. Meddars." Kelli smiled teasingly. "Lord Ravon is attractive, but—" An enthusiastic Ammie interrupted the conversation and they never finished it.

It took an hour to get to the part of the city where Lord Travalla and his wife Lady Nellandra lived. New sites and smells beckoned on every corner, and as they passed, many Shamaru turned to stare. Some bowed respectfully, but others turned their eyes away.

Boarding a train, they traveled via the tunnel shuttle, and came out on the opposite area of the mountain city. There were many chiseled marble verandas in this affluent section of the city. Lord Ravon led the way toward the highest, most elaborate entrance, a suitable residence for the ruling family of Shamar. The mansion impressed Kelli, but it made her fear that such a wealthy, powerful family might not welcome her.

The doors swung open and Lady Nellandra herself greeted them. The first thing that struck Kelli was that her grandmother, Lady Nellandra, was not winged, and wasn't a Shamaru. Kelli hesitated. This wasn't what she expected. It took a moment to realize Lady Nellandra was a Nellari. She should have made that connection since Galandra, the high priestess of Nellar, was her father's aunt. Her grandmother was slender, beautiful for her age, but without the traditional tattooing of her people.

"Welcome to Shamar, children. Please come in." Nellandra stepped aside to allow the group of students and teachers to enter, but did not take her eyes off Kelli. *This is my grandmother,* Kelli thought. She sensed that the woman longed to take her in her arms, to reach out to her. But the scan Galandra had done made Kelli's trust hard to gain.

"Thank you for your hospitality, Lady Nellandra." Michael Gentry presented the gifts of greeting, customary for guests to give their hostess on arrival. Shual had helped select the gifts from their cargo. These were wind chimes in the shape of birds made of colored glass and silver, and the last two chocolate bars from Klaus's stash.

At first Nellandra didn't know what to do with the wind chimes, but soon became overjoyed when shown how they jingled when hung in front of an open window. She assured the students that she would have the chimes hung where she could listen to them as she meditated.

The chocolate was easier. The smell told Nellandra they meant her to eat it. She broke off a small bite and put it in her mouth. "Mmm, delicious," she said, and smiled. After Nellandra accepted the gifts, she led the group down the hall to meet Lord Travalla.

***

Travalla had seen Kelli once from a distance when he sat as head of the Council of Unity. Now he scrutinized her to see if she was the daughter of his son. Ravon had said she had the eyes of a Shamaru baby before they darkened in the intense light of Shamar, soft lavender eyes. He had also said she held herself well and had earned the admiration of the Degg, and Travalla's sister-in-law Galandra. Lord Travalla nodded his approval. She did not know he thought Ravon would find in her a good wife and mother for his children. The thought that she might refuse such an honor never entered his mind. His son Holba had not lived to inherit the house of his ancestors. He wanted to make sure his great-grandson would.

Kelli extended her hands as her turn came to greet Lord

Travalla. Instead of returning the normal greeting, Travalla pressed her hands to his face and held them there.

"Forgive me, you bring back painful memories. In time, your presence will become a comfort. I am so glad you came." The emotion was powerful and the words sincere. She realized that Lord Travalla was shaking. Their meeting overwhelmed him. "Forgive me, Nellandra is the emotional one. She cried when she learned about her granddaughter, and fretted about this meeting." He shook his head. "She is holding up well, while I am behaving like a blubbering old fool."

***

"I thank you for seeing me," Kelli began, and then disregarding protocol, she threw her arms around his neck and planted a kiss on his cheek, as she used to kiss her father when he came home from a trip. There were tears in both their eyes when she let go. "That's an old Earth custom."

"Then our worlds have much in common," Lord Travalla answered. "We have much to talk about, but there is no hurry."

Kelli followed the others into a spacious dining hall where they would enjoy their meal. She saw tables laden with more food than they could eat in three days. The delicious aroma made Kelli realize she had not eaten since early morning. Duncan was already helping himself to the spicy meat that he had enjoyed on the Bengari vessel.

After the meal, Lord Travalla invited Duncan and Michael to join him in his chamber, which served as an office. The other students went exploring with three young Shamaru as guides. Lady Nellandra declared herself worn out from the excitement, and then suggested Kelli might like a tour of the city. Lord Ravon offered to show her around.

"Thank you." Kelli smiled, puzzled by his apparent eagerness to see to her enjoyment of Shamar. "Where do you suggest we begin?"

Lord Ravon gave her what looked like a mischievous

smile. "If we go into town, we'll run into the others. If you're up to a little adventure, we can ride bravels up to the misty gorge. If we leave now, we can make the afternoon lights."

"I don't know if I should leave the city," Kelli said. "How late will it be when we get back?"

"Are you afraid?" Ravon challenged. His eyes sparkled with amusement. "I assure you it will be safer than traveling across the galaxy."

"Of course not. I don't want to worry the others by being gone too long," Kelli replied, smiling. She was up for a little fun and adventure. "What are bravels?"

"Bravels are the fastest animals on Aldebar, and Lord Travalla has a stable of prime racers here." Ravon laughed at the startled look on her face. "Don't worry, I'll find you a gentle mount."

What bravels are, Kelli said to herself when they arrived at the stable, *is huge*. The creatures looked like a cross between an eagle and a mountain lion, and they were the size of a gigantic horse. Their wingspan was enormous. She didn't like the look of those claws, but apparently, their disposition didn't match their ferocious appearance. Lord Ravon greeted them by name, and they stood as he stroked first one and then the other.

Kelli jumped when she felt a sudden nudge in the middle of her back, to find a large golden bravel standing behind her, its head hanging dejectedly.

"You've hurt her feelings," Lord Ravon laughed. "Saba was trying to be friendly. She is one of Travalla's best animals, but she is not one who normally takes to strangers. Consider yourself privileged."

Kelli looked at the enormous beast. Saba's head was down, and she was making the most pitiful moaning sound. Kelli stroked her golden wing feathers. "I'm sorry. You surprised me. Would you like to take me for a ride?"

Saba's head shot up. When Kelli looked into the bravel's

yellow eyes, she imagined Saba had understood her. When she looked at Ravon, he nodded.

"If you're riding Saba, I'll need to take Bar." Ravon moved toward a smoky gray bravel. "He's the only thing faster than she is."

"Is she safe?" Kelli asked, not wanting her impulsive choice to put either of them in danger.

"Oh yes, quite safe," Ravon responded. "It would crush my pride if you left me in the dust on your first ride, nothing more."

Kelli laughed at the translator's choice of metaphors. Hundreds of feet up in the air, they would disturb more clouds than dust, unless you counted the tiny dust particles present in the atmosphere. She saw the puzzled look on Ravon's face and tried to explain. Once he understood, they both laughed and speculated on other gaffs the translator might make. It showed Kelli a different side of Lord Ravon, one that she liked.

When she mounted Saba, Kelli's nerves returned. She perched on the bravel's back, her legs strapped behind Saba's wings. Ravon laughed and helped her adjust herself so she was sitting up with her legs underneath her in the stirrups. Saba bore this all without fidgeting. Ravon rewarded her with a chunk of raw meat.

They were off, and flying brought a rush of exhilaration that Kelli had never experienced before. Ravon's mount took the lead and Saba followed. Kelli looked at the valleys below and the mountain peaks that loomed ahead like a vast maze, realizing that if she lost sight of Ravon, she could never find her way back. She concentrated on closing the distance between them.

The maze of mountain peaks now stretched ahead and behind them. Circling, Ravon headed into a group of peaks. There ahead was a huge cavern in the side of one peak, and he guided his mount toward that area. Kelli followed and landed moments behind him, passing through a lite mist before reaching the shelter of the cavern. She slid off Saba. There were some tables scattered throughout the cavern, almost like a picnic area. The spot would have provided a splendid view of the mountain range, but another peak stood in front of the cavern, blocking out everything else.

"You ride well. We made it here in record time," Ravon said, admiration in his voice. "We should have a spectacular view today; the sky is clear, and the mist is heavy."

"I could throw a rock and hit the other peak, it's that close," Kelli commented, stroking Saba's magnificent head. It was a long way to come to see the side of a mountain.

"It's not as close as it appears. I brought wine and some bread; would you like some?" Ravon opened a bag tied to Bar's side. He pulled out a tablecloth, wine, glasses, bread, and fruit.

Evidently this was not as spontaneous an outing as he had led her to believe. She took the glass, thinking again that perhaps she should have told Michael or Duncan where she was going and with whom.

The sun, Aldebaran, appeared to set in the north, which brought its rays in line with the angles of the lower mountain peak. This mountainside was predominately crystalline. It reflected the light straight through the mist and into the cavern. The light, broken twice, first in the crystals and then in the mist, produced quite a display of colors. It was like being inside a collapsing rainbow, whose fragments were floating down around them. The light display lasted about twenty minutes, and neither uttered a word until the magic ended.

"That was beautiful," Kelli breathed. "It put any laser light show I've seen on Earth to shame, I can't believe it is a natural phenomenon." She sipped on the wine and listened as Ravon explained once the Shamaru thought this cavern was magical.

They headed back, going slower because it was dark and more dangerous navigating the mountain maze. Kelli held tight to Saba's reins to keep from falling off. The bravel's flight was so steady Kelli could have taken a nap in the saddle. Ravon guided Bar, and Saba stayed close behind. When they reached the stables, she slid to the ground before Ravon could help her dismount. Patting Saba's side, she thanked her for being such an excellent mount. Ravon led each bravel to their stall and made sure they had water and food.

"I need to get cleaned up before the high meal," Kelli said, and gave her clothes a shake.

"We've missed that, but Nalandra always has something to eat in the kitchen. I'll meet you there after I change into clean clothes."

"I think I'm too tired to eat. I want to get clean and sleep," Kelli laughed. "Thanks for a lovely day."

Ravon agreed. "It was nice, as was your company."

Kelli turned and headed toward her room.

"Have a nice time on your date?" Duncan inquired as he passed her in the hall.

Apparently, Lady Nellandra had known not to expect them back for the high meal, and everyone knew she had spent the day alone with Lord Ravon. Kelli went to bed puzzled about why Ravon had apparently prearranged the outing, and annoyed at Duncan for blaming her for enjoying the day. And she had enjoyed the adventure, Saba, and Lord Ravon.

Duncan apologized the next day, but there was a distance between them. Kelli could feel his tension when Lord Ravon joined their group activities, which was often.

"Are you going to break Dr. Meddars' heart?" Ammie asked gravely one morning when Lord Ravon was planning to join them on a tour of the stone mines.

"What are you talking about?" Kelli responded. Ammie was too observant, and too quick to make assumptions.

"You're spending a lot of time with Lord Ravon, and if you haven't noticed, Dr. Meddars has feelings for you." For someone so young, Ammie had a remarkable understanding of relationships. "Lord Ravon is handsome, but he won't be going back to Earth with you, Dr. Meddars will."

"Thank you, Counselor Franks," Kelli answered, and then grew serious. "Three years is a long time, Ammie. We've been here four months. From what I've seen of Aldebar, I might want to stay."

"Poor Duncan," Ammie replied sagely, then hurried away before Kelli could correct her for using Dr. Meddars' first name.

Visiting with Lord Travalla's family was enjoyable. The students had the freedom of the house, and they planned activities with young Shamaru. Kelli began packing her things for the return to Rishal the next day. It was late, and she had already said goodnight to the others when there was a beep on her message console. The sound surprised her. As far as she knew, none of the students could leave messages on the system. Assuming it must be from one of her grandparents, she pressed the recall button.

"Meet me in the stables, we need to talk." It sounded like Lord Ravon's voice. He seemed rushed, even tense.

Kelli looked at her reflection in the mirror. She couldn't go in her nightclothes. She grabbed the first thing handy, a green shirtdress, and pulled it over her head. As she left, she grabbed a piece of fruit for Saba, who would have preferred meat.

The stables were dark and silent. If Ravon was anywhere around, he was trying to hide. Kelli flicked on the light and walked over to Saba's stall. She didn't see the Darro assassin until it was too late. She was no match for the three-hundred-pound warrior, but she put up a struggle. Saba was ferocious as she fought to free herself and help Kelli.

***

The Darro stunned the great golden bravel. It was over in minutes. Once Kelli was unconscious, the Darro tied her and threw her over his shoulder, like a bag of feed. Heading for the rear entrance, he stepped too near Bar, who appeared to be sleeping. The bravel landed a solid blow, knocking the Darro to the ground. Whirling around, the assassin stunned Bar. Blood dripped from the gash on his shoulder, but worse injuries had not stopped him before. He would survive.

***

Saba's roar echoed as she threw herself against her stall. An alarm sounded as she broke free. Soon people hurried from everywhere, servants, students, Lord Travalla, Duncan, Michael, and Lord Ravon, still in their nightclothes. Wisely, they backed away when they saw Saba's fury.

"Get the tranquilizer!" Lord Travalla shouted to a servant. His bravels were high-spirited, but had never been dangerous before.

"Kelli has a way with Saba; perhaps she could help calm her," Lord Ravon volunteered. He had rushed down, fearing the house was under attack.

"She's not in her room. I went there when I heard all the noise," Liesel volunteered. "I couldn't find her."

A look passed between Lord Travalla and Lord Ravon. "Search the house. That alarm was loud enough to wake the dead."

"Has something happened to Kelli?" Michael demanded.

Duncan rushed back to the main house and returned with the news that he could not find her anywhere. "There was a message for her to meet you here in the stables." He glared at Lord Ravon.

"I left no message. I was with Lord Travalla most of the evening, then I went to my room." Lord Ravon felt an icy wave of fear engulf him. Something very wrong had happened to the Earth woman, and he was being framed.

"Look over here, there's blood." A servant got around Saba. The bravel had calmed without tranquilizers.

"Kelli." Duncan lunged toward the servant. Lord Ravon grabbed him before he got in Saba's range.

"No, it can't be, my lord Travalla. I'm afraid this here is Darro blood," the servant answered, holding some bloody straw to his nose. "I was with the border police, and I'd know that smell anywhere."

"Darro? We do not allow them inside Shamar." Lord Ravon's eyes narrowed.

"Turn Saba loose. She must have tried to stop whatever happened."

As soon as the bravel had an open lane to the door she stopped howling and took off, leaving no doubt she had scented something and was in pursuit. Lord Ravon jumped on Bar, noticing the blood on Bar's claws. "So, you're the one that gave that Darro a Shamaru welcome. Find Saba, Bar; let's get Saba."

Ravon pushed Bar, hoping to catch up to Saba. It would be several hours before the sun came up. If the Earth woman were in the hands of the Darro, she would be dead long before then, if she weren't already.

***

Back in the stables, Lord Travalla was trying to calm his guests and his wife. "We have a treaty with the Darro. There hasn't been a border clash in over ten years, and they haven't invaded Shamar since the end of the Great Wars before my grandfather's time. I'll call their representative and find out what he knows."

Everyone moved from the stables into the main house, sleep long forgotten. Lady Nellandra ordered a lite meal prepared for those who didn't want to go back to bed. Lord Travalla ordered the patrol to begin a search. Duncan and Michael both offered to go, but trying to navigate the mountain peaks in the dark with jet packs was dangerous and pointless. They would hold back the patrol or get lost or injured themselves.

"You're a seer, and a special friend of my granddaughter. Do you sense anything that might help the searchers?"

Lady Nellandra's voice brought Duncan's mind into focus. His panic and concern for Kelli had blinded him to the one area of help that he could offer. The look in Nellandra's eyes said that she had tried and failed, though as a Nellari her psychic ability was far greater than his. Duncan focused to empty his mind and concentrated on an image of Kelli's face. It was faint at first, but it was there.

"She's alive," Duncan whispered as he struggled to maintain the fragile link. "I can't tell where she is, but I can feel the cold. She's freezing and in great pain."

***

The assassin dumped Kelli's limp body in the snow and ice. He checked the fuel gage on his jet pack. Enough fuel remained to get him across the border and out of the Shamaru homeland. This was the spot the Narr lord had directed him to. He found the bundle nearby and picked it up. He took a torn robe from the bundle and swiped it across Kelli's face, smearing it with her blood, still oozing from a broken nose. The robe belonged to Lord Ravon. The knife he would use to slit her throat also belonged to the Shamaru lord. His instructions had been clear. Following an ancient Shamaru form of execution, he would kill the Earth woman and hang her feet first from the cliff. There was to be little doubt that Lord Ravon had committed the murder.

It was time to finish the business. Tying her feet together, he pulled her up by the ankles. Once she was hanging in the proper position, one easy stroke would drain the life from her body.

Saba's golden eyes watched; watched and waited. She remembered the effects of the stun weapon. Her predator instincts told her to strike when the Darro was vulnerable, when his hands were away from the weapon. His back was to Saba now, his weapon hanging uselessly from his side. She struck, lunging at the Darro, and pinning him with her weight. Sharp claws and teeth viciously tore her victim to pieces.

Lord Ravon, riding Bar, arrived to find Saba standing over the dead Darro's body.

He could see Kelli hanging behind Saba, but couldn't tell if she was alive. He dismounted and approached Saba, bringing her mate Bar with him. Saba walked toward Bar with her head down. Lord Ravon rubbed her head, murmuring words of endearment. He walked over to Kelli, cutting her down. She was alive; bruised, battered, and with internal injuries, but alive. There wasn't much he could do for her here, except put some warmth in her body. His communicator was still on Bar. He got it and called for help. Her body was shivering—hell, he was freezing himself, and he was wearing a thermal robe. He looked around for something to start a fire, but nothing was dry enough and he didn't dare move her. She had been in the cold so long. Lord Ravon lay down and covered Kelli with as much of his body as he dared. The shivering stopped, and they lay quietly for a while, waiting for help.

When the patrol arrived, Lord Ravon moved to make room for the stretcher. They strapped Kelli in and hoisted her up to the hovering rescue vessel. Ravon turned Bar and Saba over to one of the patrol, and joined Kelli in the hovercraft's warmth. A medic took a blanket and began rubbing the snow and ice from Ravon's wings.

"How is she?" Ravon fidgeted under the ministrations. His eyes watching as other medics worked over Kelli, who had not regained consciousness.

"It's hard to tell. None of us is familiar with human physiology." The answer from the medic was brief, his voice troubled. "I think she is suffering the effects of a drug and having suffered quite a beating."

"There are other humans at Lord Travalla's, but the Darro targeted her." Lord Ravon reported to Lord Travalla using the transport's communicator. "Someone has discovered her identity and wanted to use her death to destroy me."

"And me," Lord Travalla agreed. He called his personal physician, skilled in both Shamaru medicine and the use of Nellari healing stones. Everything was ready when the hovercraft carrying Lord Ravon and Kelli landed.

Lord Ravon jumped out of the craft, followed by the stretcher carrying Kelli. They lowered it to the landing pad and rushed forward. The students were in a state of panic when they saw Kelli's bruised condition.

"What happened? Who did this? Why would anyone want to hurt Kelli?" Duncan's confusion and pain turned to anger.

"A Darro assassin almost killed her. We don't know why," answered Lord Ravon.

"Someone pays assassins. Can you find out who is behind this?" Michael's voice was cold, controlled. He put a comforting hand on Duncan's shoulder.

"Not from the Darro, Saba got to him first." Lord Ravon could understand their concern, their anger. He wished he had more answers.

The news from the doctors was good; a broken nose, a few cracked ribs, nothing that wouldn't heal.

***

Behind closed doors, Travalla met with his wife and Lord Ravon.

"I don't want to put my granddaughter in more danger," Lord Travalla began. "Perhaps the safest thing would be to send her back to Earth."

"Are you forgetting the shuttle explosion?" Lord Ravon was pacing the room, alarmed both by the attack on Kelli and his emotional reaction to the thought of her leaving Aldebar. "Publicly acknowledging her as a member of your family before the council will offer some protection."

"Don't you think you should consult my granddaughter before you make such an announcement?" Lady Nellandra commented dryly.

Three days passed before the doctor felt Kelli had recovered enough to deal with visitors. They propped her up with pillows in a sleeping chamber near that of Lady Nellandra, who had insisted on acting as her personal nurse. The room had once belonged to Kelli's father. She attempted a smile when she saw who her first visitor was.

"Your face looks better," Lord Ravon volunteered

"Better than what? I have a busted lip, a broken nose, and a black eye," Kelli laughed. She nodded to the chair next to her bed. "Please sit down."

"You're feeling better too," Lord Ravon continued, sitting down. "Are you ready to talk about what happened?"

"I think so. Do you know why anyone would want to attack me? There was a message to meet you in the stable," Kellie said.

"I didn't send that message, but someone wanting to frame me did." Lord Ravon rubbed his hands together. This was harder than he had imagined. He had planned to take his time, charm, and woo her before proposing marriage. "For many years, the Travalla family has led Shamar and her people well. When your father died, everyone thought the family line died with him. Lord Travalla was too old to have more children. He has prepared me to take over when he steps down. Not everyone is happy with that choice. They were even more upset when you arrived."

"What kind of threat could I be? I've read some of your laws, and I can't inherit his position. I wasn't born in Shamar."

"But your son could and would, if he were born here."

Sudden understanding dawned on Kelli. It explained everything. The visit, Lord Ravon's behavior, and the times he had arranged for them to spend alone. "Was I about to receive a proposal then?"

Shamaru don't blush. However, Ravon looked as if he'd rather face down ten armed Darro than meet her angry violet eyes. "It is what Lord Travalla wishes and what Shamar needs."

"My grandfather wants to use me as a tool to maintain power."

"Your grandfather honors you. The Travalla family has led

the house of Shamar for hundreds of years. His great-grandfather drafted the peace treaty that helped establish the Council of Unity. Lord Travalla loved your father very much, and wants to see that you receive your rightful place in our society."

"And you would marry me to please him?"

"For the good of Shamar, yes, and because I have found you to be an honorable woman. Someone I would be proud to have bear my sons."

The compliment took Kelli off guard. It made her stop and remember that Shamaru culture and customs were ancient, and that she had no right to judge Lord Ravon by human values.

"You honor me, Lord Ravon, and I will consider your proposal." Kelli realized she was wearing a thin sleeping gown and pulled the robe tighter. "I'm feeling tired now."

Lord Ravon nodded and left. Kelli got the feeling that a Shamaru woman would have never answered his proposal with "I'll think about it," no matter how unusual the circumstances. The strange customs of the Earth people would take time for him to get used to.

Kelli discussed the proposal with Lady Nellandra, who assured her she was a welcome member of the family, even if she did not accept Ravon's proposal. She suggested Kelli might like to tour the hall of naming, a place of family history in Shamar. There were genealogical records dating back a thousand years, and many personal records on Kelli's father. These records included a video of him growing up. Kelli accepted enthusiastically, but had to admit that it would be several days before she was in shape for such a visit.

***

After the attempted murder of Kelli in the Shamaru Homeland, Shual opened his sealed office containing the Eric program. It had become progressively more powerful, and was beyond anything he had expected. Shual acknowledged, at least to himself, that he was dreading this meeting. He switched on the computer.

There was a hesitation, as if the program were reluctant to appear. The holographic image of Eric was larger, but it stood there with its head lowered, almost cowering.

"You were gone for several days, friend Shual."

"Many things have happened. This one has been as far as Shamar," Shual explained. "There has been a terrible attack on Kelli."

"Is she...?" The lights in the room flickered, but the image did not raise its head.

"She is recovering well. Lord Ravon saved her," Shual hastened to assure the program.

The hologram brightened and appeared to solidify. Shual reached out and let his hand pass through the image. Relieved, he walked toward his workstation and inserted a new data chip. "The attacker was a Darro assassin. He failed, but there will probably be more. One thinks this is the work of Narr Lord Gorron, but we have no proof." He nodded toward the data that was loading. "That contains everything we have on the Narr lord and his people. Perhaps he has a weakness."

"Let me out and I can kill him. Nothing will connect his death to you or Kelli."

"We don't want him dead. We want to defeat him and prove that he ordered the attack on Kelli and the death of her father. It would also benefit the Narr dissidents," Shual said.

"This is what Kelli wants?"

"Yes, unquestionably. She has long sought to solve the mystery of her father's disappearance," Shual answered, and closed the program.

***

Later, Kelli received several visitors and was about to inform Lady Nellandra's maid she needed to rest when the maid announced Shual.

Her weariness evaporated, and she held out her arms to

him. Shual took her hand and bowed. He had never grasped the Earth custom of hugging.

"It is so good to see you friend," she said, patting the side of the bed. "How are you?"

Shual moved a chair close to her bed.

"This one is well, thank you." He reached in the pocket of his robe and pulled out a small device and handed it to her. "There is good news on this message, but you must destroy it once you have viewed its contents."

Kelli scooted up in her bed and activated the device. A small view screen appeared in front of her. Nalta's smiling face greeted her, and then the image drew back and she was standing in a field of tall flowers blowing in a gentle breeze. Kelli's first thought was that Nalta was somewhere in Nellar.

"Hello, Kelli. I wanted you to know that I am safe. I owe my life to you. Your friend Shual got me to a group of Narr dissidents who have colonized a moon that orbits Aldebar. The Nellari discovered the moon and made it habitable. They smuggled me here on a Bengari ship. There are many Narr here. Life is simple, but we are free. There is no assimilation." Even on the screen, Nalta's skin seemed to glow with happiness. The image faded and Kelli pushed the device's erase feature.

CHAPTER TWENTY-FIVE
—Aldebar Prime—Degg Homeland

The second marriage proposal came one day after Kelli's return to Rishal. Though she knew that Duncan's feelings for her were sincere, she also knew the recent events in Shamar had prompted his proposal. Neither of them had said anything of marriage. It complicated her feelings for Duncan. He was a wonderful man, her best friend, and she found him attractive, but marriage was something else. Somehow, she kept coming back to the fact that Duncan was human, and she was not. If she married him and returned to Earth, would they be able to live a normal life? Knowing some factions of the UNWL, she had little doubt that Duncan's career would be the price he would pay for their marriage. When she told him as much, he said she was talking nonsense. In the end, he got the same answer as Lord Ravon, and liked it even less. She would think about it, and when the time was right, she would decide when and whom she would marry.

News of her identity spread among the students at the open school. Wherever she went, a chorus of whispers followed her. It divided the students by their reaction. Some resented the fact that they were among the last to know, and felt that she had lied to them. It excited others, and they stood firmly behind their friend.

The students weren't the only problem Kelli needed to deal with. Shual reported no progress in disarming the protection function in Eric. Dr. Gentry had advised him to leave Eric deactivated, but he wanted to discuss it with her first.

"I guess I can get the real Eric to fix it when I get back to Earth," Kelli replied. "If I go back to Earth."

"One hates to lose the opportunity to work with Eric," Shual answered, not commenting on the decision his human friend was debating. "This one needs Eric's help to prove a theory that may explain the shuttle's explosion."

"I went over every aspect of the shuttle trip in Eric's records," Kelli answered, and then realized that Shual was aware of that and he must mean something else. "What can I help you with?"

"It is a theory, and one hesitates to discuss it." Shual's hand stroked his new peace stone inside his robe. It was pale blue, while hers was still orange and purple. His action was enough to let anyone familiar with his behavior know that something troubled him.

"Go ahead, no one can hear us here, and I think you know you can trust me."

"Well, Miss Royal, there may be a link between the shuttle explosion and the attack on you with another incident that occurred many years ago." Shual stopped there. He waited to see if Kelli would make the connection. He saw a glimmer of comprehension and continued. "This one's research shows that the authorities did not properly investigate Lord Holba's death. From what one can surmise, the medical staff was more concerned with the possibility of an alien virus infecting Aldebar than with the actual nature of Holba's illness. They came to a very hasty judgment, which has at least a possibility of being wrong."

"Are you saying that someone murdered my father?" Kelli asked, considering Shual's comment.

"That is a theory that this one is at present investigating.

Lady Galandra agrees there is a possibility."

Kelli gasped. If Galandra shared his fear, it was almost certain to be so. "How can Eric help you?"

"I understand he contains quite a catalog of Earth data, genetics, etc. I hoped we could use his data bank to identify the toxin responsible for Lord Holba's death." Shual paused for a second. "I have acquired the medical files, which have a sample of Holba's blood taken just before he died."

"Do what you think best. I trust your judgment more than my own." Kelli stretched her tired muscles. "There is one more function that you may find useful. Eric can break through most security programs and access classified files without being detected."

"Interesting, but also illegal on Earth and Aldebar, I believe." Shual shook his head. "Suppose they had caught you?"

"They would have offered me a job with the government," Kelli answered flatly. "They need the help."

"Disrespecting authority is no joking matter, Miss Royal," Shual chided. "One loses all hope of seeing the true colors of your stone emerge."

Kelli recognized and appreciated Shual's dry humor. She knew he would never pass judgment on her. He wouldn't even advise her about Lord Ravon's proposal, and she would have preferred someone else make that decision.

Lord Travalla and Lady Nellandra were going to introduce her as their granddaughter in a few weeks, and she felt she owed Lord Ravon an answer before then. A trip to the Hall of Naming might help her decide.

Kelli wished she could go alone, but although the tour would be private, Lord Travalla insisted she have armed guards everywhere she went. In fact, she had literally tripped over a guard sleeping in the hall in front of her room, and those were the physical guards. She did not know what kind of electronic surveillance they had installed to ensure her safety.

To get to the Hall of Naming, she once again traveled to the Shamaru homeland. The hall had been closed to all other visitors, so she was free to walk from room to room and spend as much or as little time as she wished in each area. They dedicated the whole first floor of the building to the history of Shamar. It would take months to put a dent in all the material. On the next level, which was down not up because they built the hall into one of the largest mountains in Shamar, there were rooms dedicated to the genealogies of the most prominent families. The Travalla family, being chief among the ruling families, had a large room on this floor.

Kelli spent hours in that room. She looked at holograms of ancestors hundreds of years old. There were videos of her father growing up. Lady Nellandra had lovingly preserved school pictures and photos of family trips and placed them in the hall. There was a video of the funeral. Kelli watched with tears washing down her cheeks.

Her father's funeral was a formal Shamaru ceremony. It began with a parade from the house of mourning to the funeral pyre. Everyone dressed in white and followed the body to the Spirit Cave. This, according to Shamaru law, was the highest cave on the highest mountain in the homeland. They had recorded each detail of the ceremony, and Kelli battled tears as she watched. After praising the deeds of the deceased, Lord Holba, they burned his body as wind from fans blew his ashes out over the homeland.

They presented Lord Travalla with a ceremonial box, which would have contained three of his son's feathers if Lord Holba had inherited the Shamaru wings. It contained instead a lock of his hair and his peace stone. The box and its contents were behind what looked like clear glass in the hall.

The sound of Kelli's anguished sobs so alarmed the guard discreetly stationed outside the door that he used his communicator to call the home of Lord Travalla. Lady Nellandra thanked him for his concern, and advised that he should let Kelli cry out her grief. It was what humans do, she explained, since there were no grief stones on Earth to ease the pain of loss. In fact, according to all reports, there were no living stones on Earth at all. The guard shook his head in disbelief and turned back to his post. The crying was softer now.

***

Kelli left the hall at peace with her father's memory for the first time. She also knew that she would remain on Aldebar. The hardest thing now was telling Duncan her decision. He deserved to be the first to know. It would affect his life as much as her own. After Duncan, she would call Lord Ravon.

"Are you crazy? Someone tried to kill you," Duncan fumed. "We should send you straight back to Earth, for your own safety." His reaction to her news was one of anger and hurt.

"I wouldn't describe my life on Earth as being safe."

"So now you're going to marry Lord Ravon, but you can't look at me and say you love him."

"I haven't known him long; love might come in time. Besides, I'm not marrying him for love," Kelli replied. It tore at her heart to hurt him.

"Did you forget about us? Are you going to say now that you don't have feelings for me?" Duncan demanded. "I know better than that, if you don't."

"I'll always care for you, but it's not enough," Kelli replied. "Sometimes you must do the right thing, even when it means giving up something you love. Marrying Ravon is the right thing for me to do. Don't ask me to explain why, I can't. I just know this is right."

They argued for hours. Duncan never understood and never persuaded Kelli to change her mind. They did not hug goodnight. It would take time to mend their bruised feelings. Kelli had difficulty going to sleep. When she did, her dreams were as turbulent as her emotions.

***

Kelli met with Lord Ravon and things went better. He was getting the answer that he wanted, or at least most of what he wanted to hear. They met in Shual's office. Kelli felt shy. She had known Lord Ravon for a short time, and here she was about to agree to marry him.

"I gathered from your message that you have reached a decision." Ravon's tone was gentle. He must have reviewed reports of her trip to the Hall of Naming.

"I have given it great thought, and if you are still willing, it would honor me to marry you," Kelli answered. She hesitated before adding, "If we can agree on certain conditions."

"Conditions?" Ravon sputtered. "Is this another Earth custom, that a man must agree to conditions before he can take a wife?"

"No, but this will not be a typical marriage." Kelli struggled for the right words. "This is what we once called on Earth, a marriage of convenience. We don't know each other."

"If you doubt my sincerity, Shamaru view marriage as a sacred union. There is no such thing in my homeland as divorce."

"I don't doubt your sincerity; you are an honorable man. You helped save my life." Kelli fidgeted with her robe. "I want to fulfill my obligations to my friends. I agreed to attend the open school for three years. Until that time is up, I would like to remain there."

"Three years is a long time, but some of that time has passed. Is that your condition?"

"It's a big condition. I meant it as no offense," Kelli answered.

"As you say, we need to know each other. Perhaps it is better to be open about conditions and expectations," Lord Ravon said, not sounding offended. "You will be a faithful wife?"

"You have my word."

"After your three years is up, you will remain on Aldebar

and live with me in Shamar?" Ravon's eyes narrowed. "Even when the others leave?"

"Yes, I've already discussed my plans with them."

"You will never try to take our children and return to Earth?"

"Only if my husband goes with us for a visit."

"I am happy we agree on this." Ravon smiled at the woman he would soon marry.

Kelli's nervousness was all too apparent.

Ravon laughed. "You're trembling, but I would wager that you could haggle with a Bengari merchant and hold your own."

He knew about her relationship with Duncan and that she had given that up, and her life on Earth, to honor her father and his people. He whispered, "I am not without feelings, Kelli. If ours is not a marriage of love, perhaps it will become one of friendship."

CHAPTER TWENTY-SIX
—ALDEBAR PRIME—DEGG HOMELAND

A year had passed since Kelli had arrived on Aldebar. While she would remain in Rishal for two more years, her safety made delaying the marriage impossible. The day arrived and Lady Nellandra adjusted the straps on the marriage dress. They had purchased the finest purple gauze in Nellar for the gown, and it was beautiful. She could not have dreamed of more loving grandparents.

"I know this is too revealing for your comfort, but you will wear an elaborate feather cape over it through most of the ceremony." When the straps were in place, she added, "You look lovely."

Nellandra realized how nervous Kelli was about the Shamaru marriage rites. Little by little she had made a psychic link with her granddaughter, careful not to force her mind into Kelli's. Kelli showed little psychic ability, but in the future, that could emerge. Humans were uncomfortable about having their thoughts read. Dr. Meddars had even explained it was not uncommon for humans to fear and persecute those with psychic abilities.

***

Across the city, Shual dressed in fine new robes of silver

and black to prepare for the marriage of Kelli to Lord Ravon. It was to be a small, elegant wedding with nothing leaked to the press. He placed his hand on the door to his secured office. Perhaps one should tell the Eric program of the event.

"Friend Shual, Lord Rom is waiting. It is time to go." Cort, his personal assistant's voice, came from the front room. Shual gasped and hurried to join them. He did not notice the light warning that he had activated the unlock sequence. All he thought about was that in three hours Kelli would be Lady Ravon.

***

"I should have waited to get dressed." Kelli's palms were wet. Bonding material was blood, feathers, and hair from the bride and groom. These were burned together to symbolize the union of two families. "On Earth couples have their blood tested to be sure they come to the marriage free of disease."

"Humans are practical then. I like that. You must tell me more about your world," said Nellandra.

The conversation ended there, for the Shamaru priest arrived. After greeting Lady Nellandra, he got to work. He clipped a handful of hair from Kelli's curls and, using a razor-sharp ceremonial knife, he made a slight cut on her shoulder. Blood flowed into the small bowl. It was over in a few minutes, and Nellandra pressed a cloth soaked in anesthetic to the cut.

"It will heal." She stroked Kelli's hair. "We must go now; the guests will be waiting."

The wedding was to be a mixture of Shamaru, Nellari, and Earth customs. They would observe the Shamaru marriage rites, including the blood ceremony. Galandra had insisted on blessing the couple and granting Kelli Nellari citizenship. Her children would inherit the citizenship. Her sister's generous gift brought tears to Nellandra's eyes. She had given up her citizenship to marry Lord Travalla.

Kelli insisted Michael escort her down the aisle, and her

female friends would serve as bridesmaids.

Unknown to Kelli, Lord Ravon had conferred with Michael, and a week prior to the wedding had presented her with a beautiful engagement ring. Touched by his thoughtfulness, she had rushed to find a wedding band for him. Having the ceremony on Earth was out of the question. After much debate, they decided to have the wedding in Rishal. The high lord of Deggar provided a large banquet hall for the ceremony. Lush tropical flowers from the Nellari homeland transformed the room into a tropical garden, thanks again to Galandra. By Earth standards it was indeed a small wedding, only fifty guests. It was, however, quite lavish, in keeping with the status of Lord Travalla.

Kelli watched, a lump in her throat, as the feathers, blood, and hair burned on the alter, symbolizing the union of the two family's spirits. Duncan had relented and attended the wedding, giving her his blessing. Everything was going well; no last-minute mix-ups had marred the ceremony so far.

"Stand still. Do not move, or everyone dies," a gravelly voice boomed over a speaker. "We have neutralized the guards outside this chamber."

Hands went for weapons, but a wedding is a place for peace and love, not war. Heads turned, trying to locate the source of the threatening voice. Since there was no response to the emergency alarm, they had neutralized the guards, as the voice had stated. Lord Ravon signaled everyone should form a circle with the women inside. The voice was familiar, too familiar.

"We are here to dispose of the hybrid and wash the stain from the House of Travalla. Turn over the human woman and you can go free."

"This woman is my granddaughter," barked Lord Travalla. "I will not let you harm her."

"She is the offspring of your own hybrid monster. You continue to contaminate the blood of your ancestors."

Shual nodded toward a speaker in the far corner of the

room. "I recognize that voice. It seems Lord Gorron is doing his own dirty work this time."

"This woman is my wife, and I will defend her with my life." Lord Ravon stepped in front of Kelli. Duncan, Michael, and Shual joined him making a complete circle of protection. "Show yourself, Lord Gorron, coward."

"I expected as much," Lord Gorron laughed, his face appearing on the overhead view screen. "Soon I shall rid Aldebar of the entire stench you have inflicted on us. Look around, this will soon be your funeral pyre."

Lights flashed, and alarms blared. The irradiant figure of Eric appeared in the room, a full ten feet from the nearest terminal.

"I have secured this building. Surrender at once, you have no chance for escape," the hologram's voice demanded.

Judging from the distance and Eric's increased size and image, Kelli tried to guess at the cog-level Eric was functioning at. Perhaps as high as a L-12. That should be impossible.

"What trick is this?" Lord Gorron snapped. "Do you think I fear an image?"

"There is no trick. This is a sophisticated program carrying out its primary function," Shual said, then added in a quick whisper to Kelli, "Forgive me, Lady Ravon, but it seems I neglected to shut Eric down this morning."

"What files were you accessing?" Kelli whispered back.

"The Aldebarian communications network," Shual answered.

"Stop whispering. I take no orders from a computer image." Gorron was furious. Attempts by his agents to open the doors were failing, and he had revealed himself. It was too late to withdraw.

"You are in error. If you do not disarm the explosives, you will die. I have secured all exits."

"Error? You are the one who errs. I am quite prepared to die for the cause of purity." Lord Gorron's eyes burned with the glow of a true fanatic.

"Stop, Eric. Lord Gorron wants me. The others don't need to die to protect me. It's not worth it." Kelli tried to pull free of her new husband's restraining arms.

A deafening sound stilled the ensuing confusion. Lord Gorron covered his ears with twisted hands. This time Eric's simulated voice boomed as if it carried the authority of a God, reverberating throughout the room. Gorron's image was no longer on the overhead view screen. Instead, there appeared a low, ugly building surrounded by high security fences. It was a Narr compound.

"This is the Narr place of assimilation. It holds the knowledge of all who came before. The generators will soon reach overload. Unless all hostilities cease and you release Kelli, I will destroy this building and its function will end."

Gorron's howl of rage bellowed above the speakers. Eric had defeated him, and he knew it. Disregarding his orders, his men disarmed the explosives. Security teams, summoned by Eric, arrived, and crashed through the door. They took the assassins into custody. Lord Gorron's position would not protect him from punishment for his crimes this time.

Michael Gentry walked around the holographic image that had expedited their rescue single-handed. "I'm not complaining, but I thought you had deactivated his program."

"I was attempting to make some modifications," Shual explained. "I have been trying to link the death of Lord Holba to those on the shuttle and the attacks on Lady Ravon. I could increase the cognitive level, but I could not deactivate its protection function."

"Well, I, for one, am glad you failed at one task, friend." Lord Ravon laughed, which started everyone laughing, easing the tension in the room.

"If anyone has an appetite left, we have refreshments and fine Nellari wine waiting for us downstairs." Lady Nellandra spoke as if nothing out of the ordinary had interfered with the smooth running of the wedding ceremony.

Later, as guests were enjoying the sumptuous banquet Lady Nellandra had called refreshments, Duncan stood and made a toast to the newlyweds.

"To Lord and Lady Ravon, may they live long and happy lives, raise fine sons, and always do what their hearts know is right."

"An honorable man," said Ravon. He raised an eyebrow and added, "He's sitting with Lady Galandra."

Shual sat on Kelli's other side. He informed the couple, "She has invited him to spend the next school break in Nellar developing his skills as a seer."

Ravon choked and swallowed some wine to clear his throat. "That is an honor."

"She wants something," Kelli said, her eyes narrowing.

"That assumption is correct," Shual said.

Ravon laughed and raised Kelli's hand to his lips. "You are a wise woman, Lady Ravon, but let's wait to untangle that web. I wish to enjoy my wedding feast now."

The End

Teresa Howard makes her home in Hoover, Al, where shares her abode with Gracie Jane, her furry dachshund friend. She is a life-long fan of science fiction and fantasy and her dream since childhood has been to see her books in libraries and bookstores.

In 2000 Teresa participated in a Writers Workshops taught by the late Ann Crispin and has been a regular at DragonCon's Writers Track led by Nancy Knight for many years.

Though she was employed for many years as a technology coordinator and computer lab instructor in the Birmingham School System, Teresa's passions remained writing science fiction and fantasy and researching genealogy. Many of her stories have elements of both. Her work covers a wide range of speculative fiction and has been published in magazines, anthologies, webzines, and on iPhone aps in the U.S., Canada, and the U.K.

To learn more about Teresa's novels and short fiction visit her Amazon Author's page.

www.ingramcontent.com/pod-product-compliance
Lightning Source LLC
Chambersburg PA
CBHW022057170626
46808CB00002B/484